WISHING FOR
champagne kisses

This is a work of fiction.

Names, characters, places, and incidents either are the product of the author's imagination or are used fictitiously. Any resemblance to actual persons, living or dead, events, or locales is entirely coincidental.

Editing by VB Edits
Book design by Cover 2 Cover Author Services
Back Cover Photo by Cady Hennessey

www.brittaneenicole.net

DEDICATION

To my girls, you know who you are...day in and day out you support me.

Tessa is for you.

And in her words:

"Every once in a while, it's okay to put on a crown if you need a little confidence. Even if its invisible. And sometimes it's okay to wear a real one."

Thank you for being the Booktok Queens that you are.

XOXO
Brittanee

Prologue

ONE YEAR AGO

SHAWN

"Are you guys closed?"

I'm pulled out of my thoughts as a man approaches the bar, running his hands through his hair with a nervous look on his face.

"Just cleaning up, but what can I get ya?" I ask.

"Oh shit, I must look really bad if you're willing to keep the bar open on New Year's Eve," he mutters.

"Technically it's New Year's Day," I say on a chuckle, glancing back at the clock, which reads 12:45 a.m.

The guy looks down. "Ah, I'll just go home."

"No, no, stay. I'll have a drink too. I could use one after tonight."

He looks up at me gratefully. "Thanks, man. I'm Ryan Manning," he says, sticking a hand out. "I'm a firefighter with Tahoe South—just got off a long call and could use a whiskey right about now."

I hold out my hand. "Shawn Cha—" I stop myself, but it's too late, he's already put the pieces together.

"Holy shit. *The* Shawn Chase is serving me a drink. God, I'm a huge fan." His face goes from somber to fucking delighted in two seconds flat.

I shake my head, avoiding the fanfare. "Just Shawn is fine. Trying to keep a low profile."

He nods in understanding. "You had one hell of a season. Sorry about how it ended."

"Don't be," I reply in my trained way, keeping my answer short in hopes that he'll drop it. If I allow myself to think too long about what I've lost this year—my career, my life, my identity—I'll go crazy.

Ryan must sense my spiral because he quickly changes the subject. "What's with the dollars?" he asks, looking around the bar after I hand him his whiskey and clink my glass against his.

"Ah, people make wishes and put them on the dollar bills. The ladies who opened the bar—this place was their second chance, a place to start over. They wanted everyone who comes in here to think about what they'd want if they could have anything and write it down. Sort of put that energy out into the universe, I guess." I scrub my hand against the back of my head.

Second chances…I wish.

Ryan's phone rings, and he motions to it. "Sorry, I gotta take this."

I nod.

When the screen lights up, so does his face. He goes from a semi-normal guy to a man with a hundred-watt smile.

"Happy New Year, Ry," a woman cheers when he connects the video call.

"Happy New Year, Pix. How's the party?"

I try not to be nosy, but it's almost impossible with the guy sitting across from me at the bar. The woman on the other end has wild curly red hair, and she looks a bit tipsy and sweaty, but she's smiling lazily at my new friend.

"Oh, just another night out in Boston," she replies. The background noise fades a bit as she walks away from what looks like a crowd of people. "Oh, Ry, shit…Grace needs me. I'll call you tomorrow, okay?"

His smile only falters briefly. "'Kay, Tess. Please be careful."

She pauses and looks directly into the camera, giving him a saucy wink. "Is that code for don't go home with any strangers?"

WISHING FOR CHAMPAGNE KISSES

The guy squeezes the phone. His knuckles turn white, but he doesn't bat an eye. God, this is hard to watch. It's like a train wreck I can't look away from though.

"Yeah, Pix, get home safe. Give Grace my love, and I'll talk to you tomorrow."

She blows him a kiss and then the screen goes black. He stares at it for a few moments before clearing his throat when he realizes I'm still here.

"Girlfriend?" I ask carefully.

He shakes it off. "Nah, just my best friend. She's not the girlfriend type, doesn't believe in settling down. She's great though," he adds, as if he needs to defend her.

I hold up my hands. "No judgment here."

But it's obvious he wants to be more than her friend. Poor sap.

"So, about these wishes. Any good ones up there?" he changes the subject.

I take a sip of my drink, then shake my head. "We don't read them. They go up on the wall."

"What if they fall?"

"Huh?" I ask

"Can you read them if they fall?"

I shrug. "It's never happened so…"

He points to one on the ground near my foot. "Wanna do the honors?" he asks.

"Only if you replace this one with your own." I pull a black marker from my pocket and hold it out in challenge, knowing he needs to get his feelings for this Pix girl down on paper. I have a feeling if he has to think about what he really wants, he'll realize it's her.

He grabs a dollar out of his wallet and smirks, taking it in his hand and jotting down his wish immediately.

That's what I thought.

He stands up, tacks it onto the wall, and points to the dollar bill next to my foot. "Now read."

Picking up the dollar, I flip it over and laugh, recognizing the wish that was made by one of the locals a few weeks ago.

I wish for my granddaughter to find a nice man who isn't a complete toolbox. And for the hundredth time, to score with the damn niners!! Love Dolores xo

"Let's see if they get their wish…"

PRESENT DAY

SHAWN

"So the best friend just called," Bridget says to me as she cradles her bump. She's glowing, and I couldn't be happier for her.

"Who?" I ask as I look up to see *my* best friend, Ryan Manning, taking a seat at the bar. He looks stressed. I slide a coaster in front of him and grab a bottle of his favorite beer without breaking stride, keeping my focus on Bridget.

"The one who hit on you a few months ago…"

Her boyfriend—the other Ryan. Ryan Daily—laughs from his seat at the bar. "Um, baby, you definitely need to be more specific. He's Shawn fucking Chase. Who isn't hitting on him?"

I roll my eyes, and all three of them laugh, even my best friend, who has yet to crack a smile.

Bridget continues. "She came in with her girlfriends this fall, was going on about how her friend needed to get laid. She wrote on the dollar about wanting her best friend to find someone, just not you, because she was calling dibs."

WISHING FOR CHAMPAGNE KISSES

I chuckle, remembering the crazy blonde. "And what did she have to say for herself?"

"The girl had a one-night stand that night, and the guy ended up being her boss."

"No shit?" Daily says with a laugh. "That's hilarious!"

Bridget smiles at him the way only someone in love does. "Yup. They're together now. Her boyfriend even moved in with her. So everything worked out, I guess."

"Wouldn't that be nice," my best friend grumbles as he takes a sip of his beer.

I finally turn my attention to him. "What's got you so miserable?"

Ryan sighs. "My sisters are on me about bringing a date to the wedding, and I might have made a big fucking mistake."

I smile because I'm pretty sure he's being dramatic. "And what kind of mistake is that?"

He grumbles something under his breath, and we all lean in close. "I might have told them I'm dating Tessa."

My smile grows. Now this is fucking fantastic. "And why would that be a mistake?"

"Because she's coming next week, and I have to admit to my sisters that it's a lie."

"Or," I say, "and hear me out before you object—you could ask Tessa to pretend to be your girlfriend for the week and use the time to see if you can make her your real one."

He scoffs and slams his beer bottle onto the bar. "You've been reading too many romance novels, Shawn. Why would you even say something like that?"

Bridget's soft voice interjects. "Ry, you really like this girl, huh?"

Ryan shakes his head and shoots me a glare. But his icy expression melts when he looks up at Bridget. You can't be angry with a pregnant lady. It's science or something. "How 'bout when this guy admits that he's wasting his life behind a bar, I'll address that question."

I toss the rag down onto the bar and fold my arms across my chest. "Stop changing the subject."

"I will when you stop wasting your life," he counters. "Take the damn course."

"What course?" Daily asks as he and Bridget both stare at me earnestly.

Ryan scoffs. "You haven't even told them you're thinking about it? I knew you weren't serious."

My skin heats. I am serious. I just wasn't ready to share with everyone what I'd been thinking about. How watching my best friend fight fires and seeing the real good that he and the guys at the department do for our community made me think about what I wanted to do with my life. I have more money than I need. I don't need this job. But it's given me purpose over the past year.

Being a firefighter though? It would give my life purpose.

But part of me wonders if I can hack it. If my bad arm, which works well doing everything but throwing a ball, will prevent me from performing what would be required of me if I took the risk and pursued this career that has become more and more of a desire over the last few months.

Before I have the opportunity to answer, Ryan's phone rings. I look at the clock on the wall and smile. You could set your watch to Tessa's phone calls. Every night at six, which is nine where she's at, she calls him. And for fifteen minutes, he smiles. He laughs. He's an all-around lighter person.

The mask of anxiety falls from my best friend's face the second he picks up the phone. "Hey Pix," he says softly, not bothering to apologize to us for the interruption.

I turn away from the three of them, knowing that if I don't, Bridget and Daily will start asking me about the firefighter course again.

I haven't made a decision, and I don't want anyone's opinion on it until I confirm with the doctor that my arm is good to go for the strenuous training the job will require. As I grab Dailey's now-empty beer bottle and turn to throw it in the trash, a dollar literally floats off the wall. There was no gust of wind. No explanation at all as to why *this* dollar just slipped from the tape.

I sigh. Someone else is going to get their wish, and it ain't going to be me. Have to make a wish for that to happen. I lift it up, and my bittersweet mood lifts as I recognize my best friend's wish from almost a year ago.

I wish my best friend was my last first kiss.

I turn back around, the dollar in my hand, and stare at Ryan as he laughs along to something Tessa has said. For once, I can't wait to watch someone's wish come true.

Chapter 1

TESSA

"First class…" I hum as I sip my champagne in row one. I was very adamant about sitting in the first row when I spoke with the travel agent. Not because I have long legs or anything. I'm five foot one on a good day, and that's with heels. I certainly don't need the extra space first class provides. I'm compact, but I have one hell of a bite.

Nope, I need this exact row—and seat A—because my best friend Grace, the true love of my life, the Vivian to my Kit, met a total dreamboat when she sat in first class many months ago, and she was singing Fergie's lovely lyrics when it happened. Since I want to grow up to be my best friend, I'm doing everything she did in hopes that, like her, I can meet a hot stranger and have a weekend of amazing sex.

I really need it.

And by need it, I mean, in a desperate way. I have to cleanse myself of my last boyfriend. Okay, he can't really be categorized as a boyfriend, but he was a boy toy I enjoyed the hell out of until I destroyed his entire family and took my best friend down in the process.

So yeah, I'm drinking to forget all of that.

And also because I'm avoiding the reality that the first man I'll be spending time with since imploding my life is literally the greatest guy I know. He's like the male version of Grace. He's my *other* best friend. And some would say he's the one that got away. But I'd never say that. I'm not dramatic like that.

For the record, I may have had three glasses of champagne while waiting at the airport, so I'm pretty sure nothing I'm thinking right now makes any sense. "G-L-A-M," I sing shout before a man with a very round belly peeking out of his shirt sits down next to me with a grin.

Shit. So much for my palate cleanser.

Chapter 2

RYAN

"This was a really bad idea," I mutter, flipping the beer cap repeatedly in my hand.

Shawn eyes the cap, his jaw clenching, but he keeps his cool. He always keeps his cool. It drives me nuts. I'm ready to burst out of my skin, and this guy is cool as a cucumber. "And it's all your fault," I say, trying to get him riled up like me.

He just chuckles. "Just because you're nervous doesn't mean this was a bad idea. That actually probably means it was a good idea."

"And how do you figure?"

He smirks. "Means you got something to lose."

I grimace. "No shit. I could lose my best friend."

He gives me a blank stare. "Come on, you and I both know Tessa isn't the type to back away from a friend."

Gritting my teeth, I focus back on the cap. "Yeah, *friend*. That's all I should be to her."

Shawn wipes down the bar in front of me and shakes his head. "Nah, man. This is a foolproof plan. You get a test run without having to admit your feelings. If the chemistry isn't there, no harm, no foul. If it is…"

I sigh. Because it's there. It was there twenty years ago when I first laid eyes on Tessa Sanderson in a bikini. I'd known her my whole life, but then one summer, she just became more. More curves, more smiles, more touches…she became everything. And I shut down.

Because being around a girl like Tessa, someone who could flirt with an eighty-year-old widower just as easily as she could charm our teachers out of giving us a pop quiz, was nearly impossible. I didn't just want to spend a night with Tessa. One kiss would never do. She was the kind of girl who could destroy a person. With her attention, her sarcasm, and her wit.

In all honesty, I can't imagine what it would be like to have Tessa all to myself. She lights up a room, draws the eyes of everyone around her, and makes every person she comes into contact with feel special. She's like a fairy, buzzing around with her light, impossible to catch and yet drawing everyone in. Trying to get Tessa to commit to one person, to agree to be mine, felt like a foolish task back in the day. And it still is, despite what my friendly neighborhood bartender may suggest.

"I'm going to tell her I already have a date. That I worked things out with Karen."

Shawn's cheeks expand as he holds in a laugh. "Sure. If Tessa is as hot as you say she is, maybe I'll take her to the wedding."

I bite the inside of my cheek, trying to hold in the growl. The one that wants to roar out in only one syllable. *Mine.*

I'm like a damn caveman—or a toddler—ready to fight anyone who tries to take my favorite toy. Pixie. *My Pixie.*

He can't have her.

"I could take her as my date and not go through with the rest of the plan," I supply.

He chuckles. "And let your sister find out you're not dating Tessa like you told her you were last time she tried to set you up? Yeah, I'm not buying it."

After shooting Shawn a glare, I turn my gaze out to the lake. Tahoe is gorgeous in the early afternoon. Even in December. Honestly, it's my favorite time of year. The snow glistens atop the trees, the lake glitters, and there isn't a fire in sight. For an investigator on the fire department, that's a good thing. Especially when I have to be at the airport in an hour to pick up my best friend in the whole world. A call would definitely interrupt that.

I let out a sigh, accepting my fate. I'm about to fake date my best friend in hopes of making her fall in love with me. A fire is the least of my worries.

Chapter 3

TESSA

oly nips on a popsicle, it's fucking freezing! With teeth chattering, arms shaking, and my ass wiggling in an attempt to keep warm, I search the parking lot for Ryan. My lumberjack shouldn't be hard to find. He's six foot and something ridiculous, has shoulders like a mountain man, and a cock that could poke your eye out. Okay, I really don't know about that last part, but every time I've imagined Ryan's cock, it's been huge. Oh, and I'm probably still drunk. I should probably sober up before I find him and tell him how much I want to see his cock. You know, for research purposes. I want to know how realistic my dreams are. Yeah, I should definitely *not* share that with him. It'd be weird. I'm weird. And he will definitely not show it to me. Or let me live it down if I say any of this to him.

Super glad I can't find him right now. Even if I am fucking freezing.

"Where the fuck are you, Ryan Fucking Manning?"

A woman hustles her family by me, offering me a glacial glare. *Yeah, bitch, I can't feel my toes. Your mommy eyes are doing nothing for me.*

Digging my phone out of my jeans pocket, I shiver again before dialing my ex-best friend.

"Where are you?" he growls into the phone. "I'm standing at the baggage claim."

I huff in annoyance. "I'm outside. I didn't have luggage."

"It's twenty degrees out, Tessa. Why would you be outside?"

"Oh, just thought I'd get some fresh air," I pander.

He groans. "You've been here two minutes, and you're already driving me nuts."

I shimmy in my jeans, as if he can see me. "At your service."

"Get your sweet ass inside so I can hug you."

My chest warms. I sprint across the street and back into the airport in search of my grumpy best friend. As soon as I spot him, staring in the opposite direction, looking disgruntled and perfectly handsome, I drop my carry-on, sprint in his direction, and yelp into the phone, "Incoming!"

He harrumphs as he spins around, and I launch myself into his arms. I wrap my legs around his tree trunk waist, and he laughs as his hands squeeze just below my ass, pulling me tighter against him. God, that feels good.

"Hey, Pixie," he murmurs, the smile on his face growing three times its original size. My gentle giant.

"Hey, Ry," I say, staring up at him, suddenly at a loss for words. His face is cold and covered in a light dusting of hair. It's gruff enough to hurt if I run my cheek against it, yet delicious-looking enough that I consider trying. He smells like snow and fire and wood and *Ryan*. My Ryan. He's familiar and yet so different. We talk on the phone or FaceTime almost nightly, yet this is the first time I've seen him in person in over a decade. "You're bigger," I whisper, adjusting to having him this close.

"And you're still my Pixie," he says as he carries me toward my carry-on bag.

My Pixie. Gah, why does he have to say it like that? I'm thirty-six, but when he calls me Pixie, he makes me feel like I'm sixteen again, and my insides get all mushy.

Ryan leans down to grab my luggage and lifts it over his shoulder as he continues walking forward.

"You going to put me down?" I ask with a giggle.

"Nope," he tosses back as he continues his trek to the car.

22

"People are staring," I say, although I don't actually give two fucks. In fact, I like the attention. A lot. But not nearly as much as I like being in Ryan's arms.

Ryan turns to me and smirks, knowing damn well I don't give a shit about the gawkers.

Unable to handle his glacial blue eyes looking at me in *that* way, I wrap my arms around him tighter and lay my head on his shoulder, enjoying the ride. "It's really great to see you."

He breathes in, as if he's really soaking up the moment, and gives me another squeeze. "It really is, Pix."

Chapter 4

RYAN

I can't stop glancing in her direction, soaking in every moment of her presence. Tessa is finally sitting beside me, in my car, on the way to my house, for the first time since we said goodbye so many years ago.

"It's weird, right?" she says, the smile glued to her face. She's got a mouth like Julia Roberts. She's all lips, teeth, and tongue, and I can't stop staring.

I nod, my grin matching hers. "Really weird. But good."

"Ten whole days, Manning. It feels like a freaking Christmas miracle."

My lip turns up even higher. "Oh yeah? You been dreaming about me, Pix?"

She laughs this throaty and feminine and gorgeous laugh. It makes my dick stir to life, and I have to pinch the inside of my leg to stop it from growing.

"Ry, I better ease you into my truth bombs. I don't want to scare ya."

I gulp down an overeager breath. I doubt any of her truths could scare me. Besides, it's what we do. Every night we tell each other the truth. The absolute, complete truth. No matter how hard. Except I've been holding one back for years, and it's starting to feel so heavy, I can't always push it down.

"You know I always want all your truths," I say, my voice a bit gravelly.

She shrugs her shoulders, a telltale sign that her walls are climbing up. I'd love to tear them all down, along with her clothes, but now is not the time. "Oh, I've got a truth for you. Remember how I told you Grace had that amazing plane ride, which led to the most epic love story ever?"

I laugh as I nod. "Yes?"

"Well, apparently, I can't recreate my best friend's life because I drank all the champagne, sang the damn song, and even sat in the exact same seat, but a billionaire playboy didn't sit next to me!"

I'm a bit thrown that she was looking for someone like that. Money never seemed to matter to Tessa before. I quirk my brow at her. "You're looking for a billionaire playboy?"

She sighs. "Not really. I'm just trying to get over the last billionaire playboy I destroyed."

She says it as if she's teasing, but I know better. Tessa wears the guilt of what she did day in and day out. Grace forgave her, and she's admitted she didn't see a future with her ex, but despite it all, Tessa still feels guilty. She accidentally let a secret slip to a fellow reporter, and that reporter used it to break up Grace and her boyfriend. The boyfriend who happens to be Tessa's ex's brother. Although, things are better between Grace and her boyfriend now, and Grace doesn't blame Tessa for what happened. Tessa just needs to accept that forgiveness. And apparently move on from her ex. Something I thought we were past already.

"You didn't destroy them. You were all conned. And Grace forgives you. She's told you a hundred times."

She smiles, but it doesn't reach her eyes. "Yeah, I know."

I grab her knee and squeeze. "You want to see something magical tonight, or are you too tired from your non-adventure on the plane?"

She laughs. "You tease, but if I don't find someone to scratch this itch, you may find me curled up next to you in bed…and I can't be blamed for what my hands do in my sleep."

I groan, trying to cover my disappointment that she would only consider it scratching an itch. I want so much more than that. "That's not the threat you think it is, Pix," I toss back, playing her game.

Her cheeks turn a rosy pink, and she shakes her tits at me suggestively. "Bring it, big boy!"

This time, the groan isn't hiding anything. I shift in my seat and turn my eyes to the road. "You're gonna kill me over the next ten days, aren't you?"

Tessa hums beside me. "Either that, or I'm gonna fuck you. Jury's still out."

I cough out my laughter as I grip the steering wheel tighter. "Jeez, Pix, warn a guy…"

Her saucy smile hits me right in the heart. "I just did."

Chapter 5

TESSA

Ryan is *different* tonight. For years, I've flirted with him over the phone. I've toed the line with our friendship because that's who I am—I'm flirty and sarcastic, and I enjoy teasing him—but Ryan has never really reacted to it.

For a long time, he had a girlfriend—*Rebecca*. They started dating when we were in high school and continued for years after that. She made sure to keep me at arms-length from him, and I respected it. Ryan has never been interested in me like that, and I'd rather have him in my life as a friend than ruin it with sex. Sure, he's always been friendly and laughed at my flirting, and maybe sometimes he'd even flirt back, but only in a friendly way. Not like this. I don't know what *this* is, but it's *different.*

Normally, I can read Ryan like a book. We tell each other our truths. We share everything…but it feels like the man who shared all his secrets with me is missing, and in his place is this big grizzly bear who is hanging by a thread. Which is crazy. Ryan isn't like that with me. He's the guy who treats me like his kid sister. The guy who dated the tall, pretty girl in high school and rolled his eyes at me when I flirted with his friends.

With my petite frame, my curves weren't as noticeable back then, but I made up for it with my loud mouth and sarcasm. Something confident boys in school could handle. But not Rebecca. She'd whisper snidely about me under her breath. I heard her and her friends' comments loud and clear though—slut, whore, tease. Meanwhile, I was a virgin well into college, and she and Ryan were having sex at fifteen.

God, why am I going down memory lane? Especially these memories!

Right! Because Ryan is acting weird. Like any minute he could snap. Like he's holding himself together so we don't get whiplash. But I wouldn't mind a little whiplash. I've been miserable for months, trying to figure out how to help my best friend, how to properly make up for what I did to the James family, to just *be* better. I've been so preoccupied that I've lost the real me. Reckless, carefree, happy. And for the next ten days, with my *other* best friend by my side, I want to be all those things.

But I don't want to break him, and I just might if I show him all of me. If he sees the crazy parts, the things I hid because I knew Rebecca hated them, who's to say he'll like who he sees? A long-distance phone friendship has made it pretty easy to hide my faults, so what if he sees them, and it damages that friendship? What if he doesn't *like* the real me? What if I'm too much?

Clearly, I've had too much to drink because this isn't how I think. This is how Grace thinks. She overanalyzes everything. This is Ryan. We're us. Pix and the Lumberjack. It's going to be fine.

"Are you taking me to the bar to meet your famous best friend?" I tease, trying to get us back on track.

Ryan once again grips the steering wheel so tight his knuckles turn white. "You're my best friend," he says, shooting me a look I can't decipher.

"*Okay.*" I suddenly understand how Grace always feels. I'm totally in my head, and I hate it. I fumble with the radio, needing any kind of distraction. "Is your sister excited about the wedding?"

He grunts.

"Is that—a yes?"

He clears his throat as "Stellar" by Incubus plays over the speakers. I practically screech because it's one of the songs we used to drive around town blaring in high school. We loved this CD. Ryan shoots me a look as we come to a stop in a parking lot, and the smile that transforms his face takes me back two decades.

"There's my Ry," I whisper as we stare at one another, Incubus singing "Wish You Were Here" in the background, darkness surrounding the car, the engine still running, and the warmth from the radiator blowing heat straight at our faces.

But it's the warmth from within that calms me. The way Ryan is looking at me, the way we're settling back into the people we were all those years ago, and yet so completely different.

"Truth?" I offer, and Ryan nods. "It feels like no time has passed and also like you're someone I don't know at all."

His eyes caramelize, and I feel myself melting with them.

"Truth?" he rasps.

I nod, my want for his truths liquefying and making me practically float. Or maybe it's my want for him.

Or maybe it's just the alcohol.

"I think you're the only person who's ever known me at all."

The words don't make sense. We haven't spent time in the same space for over ten years. And even before that, it was sporadic because of Rebecca—she kept him on a short leash.

"How could that be true?" I ask, genuinely curious.

He shakes his head, as if it's a truth he's not ready to share, or maybe he doesn't understand it himself. He twists the key in the ignition and nods his head toward the door. "Come on, Pix. Let me introduce you to Shawn."

Even in the dark, I can see how grand Ryan's favorite restaurant is. Made up of Lincoln logs with large glass windows that wrap around the entire structure, it sits on Lake Tahoe as a beacon in the night. It's lit up against a dark sky so full of stars it looks like it was painted by Van Gogh himself.

"Holy shit," I mutter as Ryan rounds the car and takes my hand in his, tugging me forward. He's so big next to me. His hand is so large. I stare at it, almost lost in its size.

Ryan's lip tugs upward as he looks down at me. "You're being weird."

Nervous that he can read my thoughts, I nudge him with my elbow. "Just keep walking, big guy."

He laughs as he holds open the door, and I duck under his outstretched arm. Inside, the fire blazing in the large hearth is so hot it feels like the warmth of the sun on a summer day. My smile spreads wider as I soak up every ounce of this place. *Ryan's place*. The spot he's in most nights when we're texting. Where he relaxes. Where he can be himself.

"Hi, Karen," Ryan says to the hostess, who beams in his direction.

Oh, *Karen*. This is who Ryan was dating a few weeks ago. The woman he let down easy rather than inviting to his sister's wedding. The one he ended things with because he "fell for his best friend."

As in me.

Ready to play the part I agreed to, I make sure she's within earshot, then I press my body into Ryan's and say, "I can't wait to get you back to your cabin."

Ryan shoots me a quizzical look, but he squeezes me, pulling me to his side and slipping his hand under my jacket so his fingers are pressing into the flesh of my hip. The skin-on-skin contact makes it feel like the temperature in the room has risen another twenty degrees.

God, he's good at this game. Even I believe he's interested in me.

"You guys going to the bar, or do you want a table?" she asks.

I don't feel like she's giving me a look or eyeing Ryan like the snack we both know he is. In fact, she just seems kind. I back off Ryan a bit, or at least I try to, feeling bad that I was flaunting our fake relationship unnecessarily.

Ryan's grip doesn't ease up on my hip though. He holds me in place as he replies. "Bar. We're just stopping in to say hi to Shawn."

She nods in understanding, and he leads me past her and toward the bar, never letting go.

As we approach the bar, I watch as the man who has become Ryan's closest friend grimaces at every customer who walks up. For a bartender, he's not very friendly. But he is one fine specimen of a man, and if there's one thing I'm good at, it's making men smile. I pull myself away from Ryan's death grip and hop up onto a stool, flashing my wide Julia Roberts smile in his direction.

As soon as he sees Ryan, a grin replaces his scowl, and his eyes dart back and forth between the two of us. "Well, I'll be damned if it isn't Ryan's Pixie. I totally get why he calls you that now." He looks me up and down, his grin never leaving his face.

I hold out my hand in excitement. "I am so excited to meet you," I say.

As soon as the words come out of my mouth, his entire body tenses. I'm not sure what I said wrong in those few syllables, but he's completely shutting down.

"Ya know, because you're Ryan's other best friend. It's like we can fill each other in on the gaps. You can tell me about all the girls he's been dating since he hides that information from me, and I can tell you what color braces he had in the fifth grade." I nudge Ryan with my elbow, and he studies me like I'm a dinosaur at the Met.

Shawn's shoulders sag, and the smile returns to his face. "Were they bright green? I could see him rocking that and thinking it was cool," Shawn says as he slides a coaster in front of me.

Ryan sits next to me, shaking his head. "I don't think she needs anything more to drink. You hungry, Pix?"

I can't help but look between the two of them. They're just so damn gorgeous. It's like I'm a labrador and they're my new favorite toys. How can I think about food with all the hot man candy in front of me?

"Tess?" Ryan says.

I know he's talking to me, but I can't stop staring.

Shawn laughs. "I think we broke her."

I nod so excitedly I make myself dizzy. "I'm just used to Boston men who wear suits and ties...the plaid is doing something to me." I allow my eyes to roam across Shawn's chest.

Ryan slides a hand around my waist, pulling my stool so I'm between his legs. When his palm lands on my thigh, I study the way he squeezes my leg, engulfing it between his fingers.

The heat that runs through me isn't normal. Men touch me all the time. I mean, not in a sexual way, just in general. I'm used to handsy men. But they never make my pulse skyrocket the way Ryan is right now. Clearly the prosecco from the plane is still working wonders.

"I'll take a cheeseburger," I say quickly. I need to eat something so I stop looking at my best friend like he's a lumbersnack.

A snort escapes my nose, and I try to hide it, but Ryan misses nothing. "What's so funny, Pix?" he asks, inquisition in his eyes as he and Shawn study me.

"Nothing," I mutter, keeping lumbersnack to myself. He'd never get it.

"Make that two burgers," Ryan says to Shawn.

Chapter 6

RYAN

With my hand on Tessa's leg, I eat my burger and listen to her babble on about Grace's pregnancy. I swear her life revolves around other people. Whether she's reporting about someone else's life, worrying herself silly over her friends, or tending to her extremely needy family, Tessa lives for the people she loves. She's kind to a fault.

I love that for the fifteen minutes we talk at night, I force her to focus on herself. I ask questions about her life—because I want to know everything about her—and I make sure someone is checking in on her.

The ketchup on her plate is running low, so I put my burger down, grab the bottle from the bar, and squirt a generous portion in front of her, all without lifting my other hand. I'm not necessarily a handsy guy, but for some damn reason, I can't get my hand to leave her leg. It's like my body has been waiting decades to touch her, and now that she's close, I just can't stop.

"Thanks," she says with genuine appreciation as she dips her burger. I'm staring, I know it. And I need to stop. But I can't believe she's sitting here, next to me, after years of FaceTime and texts, of wishing I could give her a damn hug when she's sad or feel her laughter rather than just hear it through the phone. It's like she's a mirage I've dreamed up for all these years, and I need to keep my hands and eyes on her so she doesn't disappear.

But she keeps shooting me looks like she knows I'm being weird.

And I am.

"I'm going to run to the bathroom," she says before hopping off her stool and taking her warmth with her.

Shawn throws the bar towel over his shoulder, leans his arms against the bar, and peers over at me. "You're a fucking goner," he teases, his brown eyes lighting up as he shakes his head at me.

I groan as I rub my forehead. "I know. I told you this was a terrible idea."

He laughs as he pushes himself off the bar and grabs himself a Coke. Shawn doesn't drink anything but water most of the time. He must be tired if he's succumbing to soda.

"You okay?" I ask, happy to turn the topic to someone else.

Shawn harrumphs as he takes a sip, then places his glass on the bar. "Fine. Why wouldn't I be?"

"You've been working here for a little over a year…" I let my sentence die. I'm not sure why I'm pushing this right now.

Shawn used to be a professional baseball player. He was one of the best pitchers the West Coast has ever seen, but it all ended because of a car accident. He started working here soon after. I'm glad he's here, don't get me wrong, but sometimes I wonder if he's wasting his time. He has no family here, no real friends aside from me and the owners of the bar. It feels like his life is on hold. Although I'm one to talk. I think my life has been on hold since the day I left Tessa in Boston.

Shawn eyes me. "I'm fine. You should focus on yourself and that hot ticket you have visiting you. This is what you've been waiting for, Manning. Don't waste your time focusing on something neither of us can change." He taps the bar in a friendly manner and pushes himself away.

He's right. I need to focus on Tessa. I want to enjoy her for the next ten days. I've waited far too long to have her undivided attention like this. Before I know it, she'll be back in Boston, and we'll just be chatting again on FaceTime. I can try again with Shawn then.

As we pull up to my cabin, I hold my breath, waiting to hear Tessa's commentary on my lonely existence, but she's relatively silent. I look over and study her expression. Her lips are parted, her eyes are twinkling, and I swear if she had wings, they'd be fluttering. She looks ecstatic.

"This. Is. Amazing," she says slowly, enunciating each word.

I can't help the grin that breaks out. "Yeah?"

"Yes!" she cheers. "You're a real lumbersnack! God, it's so perfect I can't even handle it. Do you have an ax to chop wood?"

I huff a surprised laugh. "A lumber what?"

Her lips fold over on one another as she looks away from me. "Fuck," she mutters.

"Did you just call me a lumbersnack?" I inquire, giving her a smirk.

Tessa sighs. "Possibly. But you didn't answer the question. Do you or do you not have an ax?"

I keep my eyes on her as I reply. "I've got an ax."

"Care to take that shirt off for me tomorrow and cut some wood? I have a TikTok crowd that would go nuts for you," she says, her eyes lighting a fire against my skin while she gives me an unabashed perusal.

I laugh louder, the awkwardness all but gone since we left the restaurant. This is Tessa. She's not going to make this weird. She *is* weird. *She's my weirdo.* My little Pixie that says whatever comes to her mind and brings joy everywhere she goes.

"I'll see what I can do, Pix. Hold tight, I'll grab you," I say before hopping out of the truck and trudging to the other side. It's icy, and I don't want her to slip.

Before I can make it to her door, she's already opening it and huffing. "You think I can't walk, Ry? Seriously, I live in Boston. I'm used to cold weather and ice. I don't need you to—" Her voice is lost as she steps onto a patch of black ice and flies backward, landing on her ass, her head barely missing the door on her way down.

I scoop her up before she can feel the ice through her pants and pull her close as I walk toward my cabin.

"You were saying?"

She sighs against me. "Fine, I'll just enjoy my ride on the lumbersnack." She leans her head against me and nuzzles into my chest.

I laugh as I struggle for my keys. "Did you just sniff me?" I tease, looking down into her mossy green eyes, which sparkle with mischief.

"So what if I did?" she replies, never embarrassed in the least.

I shake my head on a laugh and flip on the light next to the door before making my way through my cabin to the couch.

"You know, you can put me down now. I'm not going to fly away."

She gives me a knowing look, and I place her gently down on the edge of the couch, a tad embarrassed that she called me out on it. The problem is I don't want to put her down. I don't want to say good night. But it's already late, and I'm sure she's tired.

Looking away from her, I point to the door. "I'll go grab your things. You can get settled in the bedroom. I'll take the couch."

With her hands on her hips and a loud huff, Tessa stares me down. "I am not taking your bed. And why do you only have one? This place looks big enough for another bedroom."

It is. I just never got around to setting up the guest room. It's full of gym equipment, and no one visits me that doesn't live in town. Tessa is the only person from the East Coast I keep in touch with, and my family all lives nearby. No one other than my niece stays over, and when she does, I let her have the bedroom and I take the couch. Or we build a fort and sleep in the living room. "Under the stars," as she likes to say. But since that's too many truths tonight, I ignore her and walk outside.

When I come back, I find Tessa in a corner, staring at a photo. She picks it up and looks back at me, a smile on her face. "Is this Erin?"

I nod.

"God, she's so freaking cute. I can't wait to see her in her flower girl dress."

"She's excited to finally meet Auntie Tessa."

My niece and Tessa have phone dates when she sleeps over. It happened one night when Tessa called while Erin and I were watching a movie. Tessa tried to end the call when she realized I was spending time with Erin. I shouldn't have even picked up, but I couldn't give up those fifteen minutes. And when Erin found out that I had a friend who'd known me when I was her age—eight—she wanted to know everything. They talked for over an hour while I sat with a grin on my face watching my two favorite girls interact.

Tessa lets out a contented sigh at the idea of meeting Erin. She places the photograph back down and spins around. "So it's settled."

"What's settled?"

"I'll take the couch and you'll get real rest, because, unlike me, you're on call."

I shake my head. "I won't sleep if you're on the couch."

"Well, where does Erin sleep when she stays over?"

"In my bed. I treat my girls like queens." I wink at her.

"Truth?" she offers as a blush creeps up her chest.

I nod.

"I don't think I can handle being in your bed."

I quirk a brow at her and wait for her to elaborate. When she doesn't, we stare at one another. The light from the lamp flickers—it's not magical; it does that every night, but the way it dances on and off so quickly leaves Tessa in a low glow where she stands about five feet from me.

I swallow as I consider her words.

She bites her lip and looks away from me.

"Truth?" I rasp.

She nods as her eyes meet mine again.

"I *need* you in my bed."

The light dances on and off again, and when it flutters on, Tessa is closer. Only about foot, but close enough that I can practically feel her against me, smell her vanilla scent that reminds me of high school.

I reach my hand out to pull her closer, and she allows me.

"What's happening?" she murmurs.

"We're going to bed." I look into her eyes to see if she agrees. *Am I pushing too hard? Is this what she wants?*

"Together?" she whispers, almost shyly. She's never shy. She's the outspoken girl. The girl who sasses everyone. The girl who walks into a room with sky-high heels and walks out of it with your heart. She studies me, searching my face for something I hope I'm giving her.

I wrap my hand around her waist and push my other one through her hair. "Yes. If you won't let me take the couch, we'll share the bed. If that's all right with you," I add, almost as an afterthought.

Tessa sighs and leans into my chest. "Only if you promise we can cuddle. I really like to cuddle."

I chuckle as I put my head on top of hers, drawing her in for a big hug. "We can make that happen."

Chapter 7

TESSA

Ryan lets me use the bathroom attached to his room while he uses the guest bathroom. *What the hell are we doing?* I ask my reflection, but she doesn't have any more answers than I do.

The alcohol has worn off. It's been an incredibly long day. Hell, it's been a long few months. It feels like I've been hurtling recklessly through existence ever since I blew up my best friend's life so many months ago.

Am I doing something reckless again? Sleeping in the same bed as Ryan *feels* reckless. Like it can only end in heartache. But that's if we were going into it sexually…which we aren't because Ryan doesn't see me like that. He probably has women sleep over all the time. He's a growly fireman with tree trunks for thighs and eyes that could melt a glacier. Having little old me in his bed is nothing. *We're nothing.* It's going to be fine.

Tired of overthinking and in need of a distraction, I text Grace.

Me: **How are you feeling?**

As I wait for a reply, I wash my face. I don't wear a lot of makeup, but my face is covered in millions of freckles, so wearing a little covers up a good portion of them. When my face is wiped clean, I'm left feeling like I did in middle school. Grace likes to tease me that I'm lucky I still look young, but being as short as I am with a freckle-covered face and barely any curves means I get mistaken for a high schooler more often than I'd like.

I'm the opposite of the girls Ryan dates. Rebecca was all curves and makeup. And even though Ryan and I have only ever been friends, I still wanted to kill her when he told me he'd lost his virginity to her. I'm sure there's been a trail of women who look just like her since they broke up.

Grace: **I'm fine. How are things with Ryan? Is he as hot as you remembered? Have you kissed yet? Tell me everything!**

I roll my eyes.

Me: **No, we haven't kissed. But I have a feeling we're going to need to put on an act in front of his family this week, so we should probably get it out of the way, right**?

My best friend is a matchmaker, and while her love life is a disaster—mostly my fault—I trust her judgment implicitly. And also, I'm probably looking for her to give me the okay to kiss Ryan. Even if it's just for show. It's dangerous. He's been the one constant in my life for decades. I don't want to do anything to jeopardize that. But also, I really *want* to kiss him.

I watch as the dots on the phone dance, and then finally her message appears.

Grace: **Since when are you shy about kissing a man?**

Me**: Since it's Ryan.**

Her reply is almost instant.

Grace: **Yup, the guy.**

The guy? As in my best friend. Yeah. He is the guy.

Me: **Exactly. So?**

Grace: **Just do what feels natural. It'll all be fine. And remember, you deserve to be happy.**

I frown at my phone. What does she mean by that? I am happy. Grace is always in her head, so maybe she's projecting her insane situation onto me right now.

Me: **Okay G, tell the little alien to be good to you, and when it's** second mommy is back, I'll take you out for whatever you want.

Grace: **It's a baby, not an alien. And you aren't the other mommy. Stop worrying about me, T. I love you, you ridiculous human.**

I smile.

Me: **Love you too.**

I grab my phone, my toiletry bag, and my clothes, then open the door to Ryan's bedroom. The space smells like him, and the navy bedding with the checkered red and blue flannel sheets makes me smile. It's like I've landed in Ryan World, and I can't wait to jump in. Ryan knocks on his own bedroom door.

"You decent?" he asks through the crack.

I put my stuff down on the chair and pull the door open. "Come in here, you big oaf. It's your bedroom."

Ryan is bare chested with a towel around his waist, water glistening on his muscular chest, which is covered in a smattering of hair. He's *all* man. Broad shoulders, hard edges, locked jaw, molten chocolate eyes, and his brows knit together as he stares down at me. "Where'd you get that?" he asks, pointing at the flannel shirt I'm wearing as pajamas.

I totally shouldn't fuck with him like this, but I can't help it.

"Forgot pajamas. Or more accurately, I don't wear them. Figured you'd rather me wear your shirt than be naked." I raise my brow conspiratorially, and his Adam's apple bobs up and down. "I didn't realize you'd be naked though. Should I get comfy?"

I teasingly start to unbutton the top button of his shirt, but he grabs my hand. The towel on his hip shimmies down another inch with his movement.

I want it to fall.

Fuck, where did that thought come from?

This is bad. So very freaking bad. I want to see my best friend's cock more than I'd like to admit. So much so that my thighs are clenching and my panties are damp. Needing to get away from him before I pull the towel myself, I spin around and catapult onto the bed. "Which side do you sleep on?"

Ryan stands completely still, droplets of water dripping from his hair onto his shoulders. Pretty sure he's thinking the same things I am. And while that excites me, it's also really fucking dangerous. Normally, I don't worry about feelings or how sex will affect them, but with Ryan, I have to be more careful.

I care about him. Hell, I love him. In the same way I love Grace. He's a huge part of my life, even if it's mostly virtual. He's my support system. Sex—no matter how much I need it right now—is not worth risking that.

"Did I break ya, big guy?" I tease.

Ryan shakes his head and finally smiles. It's a soft one. A Ryan one. It's the kind he gives me when he's listening to me babble on for minutes straight without taking a breath. Like he's exasperated with me but also finds my quirks endearing. I love that smile.

He clears his throat. "I'm just going to change in the bathroom. Pick whichever side you want. I normally sleep in the middle."

He disappears into the bathroom, and I fall back against the pillows, spreading out right in the middle. In the spot he normally rests his head. I can smell him everywhere. Hell, I can practically feel him.

My body aches to be touched. But I know once I start, I won't be able to stop until I come, and there isn't enough time for that.

I run my hands over my face and groan as the door opens and Ryan's bare chest once again teases me. "You didn't put on a shirt," I grumble between my fingers, peeking out at him and rubbing my legs together. This is going to be a long night.

"If I have to deal with your bare legs all night, you can suffer too," he mutters, his eyebrow lifting in challenge.

What he doesn't understand is that I'm *this* close to taking off his shirt, tweaking my nipple, and teasing my clit while he watches. I am *that* turned on. Instead, I turn over and face the wall.

A few moments later, the bed dips as he slides in, and then there's a pause before he grabs my hip and pulls me to him. "I was promised cuddling."

My lips fold in on themselves as I try to contain my smile. "Yes, you were."

He squeezes my hip twice and loops his arm around my waist. At this point, my shirt is bunched up, and when his thumb skitters against my stomach, we both breathe in.

His chest tightens, and his hand stops moving. "Is this okay?" he whispers into my ear, his voice gravelly and sexy as fuck.

I squeeze my eyes shut to keep myself from pushing his hand lower. "It's fine," I say, although it comes out more like *zz fine*. I can barely speak. I feel like a bumbling schoolgirl.

My nervousness seems to relax him because soon his hand moves a millimeter of an inch under my shirt, and his thumb grazes against my skin. "You're soft," he murmurs, and I can't help but giggle as I push myself back against him.

"See, I was just thinking you're probably hard…and I was right." He's not, but I can feel him stirring to life as my ass wiggles against him.

He squeezes my ribs with that big hand until I giggle. "Go to bed, Pix."

"Night, big guy."

Chapter 8

RYAN

Women don't sleep over. It's not something I do. I rarely date, and when I do, I don't bring them back here. This is my space to decompress. I've never even had sex in this bed. But when I wake up with Tessa's small hand running circles over my chest and look down to see her red hair sprawled across my body, as if I'm her pillow, everything feels right.

I shift her a bit to see if she's awake, but even as her hand continues to move, her eyes remain closed, and she just lets out a soft murmur of protest. She's so different like this. She's soft and quiet, so unlike the loud ball of energy that *is* my best friend. I take the time to study her freckle-covered face. I want to trace each one, spend hours counting them. I need to know how many color her face. But as I count, they blend into one another, and I know it's a useless endeavor.

Counting Tessa's freckles. What is wrong with me? If Shawn knew what I was thinking right now, he'd shake his head on a grin. "You're a goner," he'd mutter, and he'd be right. I'm so head over heels in it for this girl it's crazy.

I have to distance myself. She's only here for ten days. She'll leave, and I'll be stuck in this Groundhog Day cycle of feelings. I'll wake up wishing she was here, remember how good it felt to hold her, how right it felt when she was lying across my chest. No doubt her smell, not her perfume, but her actual syrupy scent—a cross between vanilla and drenched pancakes—is currently embedding itself in my sheets.

I rub my hand over my face and try to will myself to get out of bed. I should make a pot of coffee, start on breakfast, and maybe go lift some weights. I shouldn't lie here holding her and counting her fucking freckles. I shouldn't inhale her scent or rub my fingers across her velvet skin. But I can't help it.

As if she can hear my ramblings, Tessa's eyelashes flutter, and she winks up at me, only one eye opening. "Too loud," she murmurs.

I clear my throat. "What?"

"*Your thinking*. It's too loud. Stop freaking out and cuddle me." She presses into me and rubs her nose against my chest. I shift because it tickles, and if I'm not careful, it might make me giggle.

What the hell is she doing to me?

She wraps her legs around my hips and sits up so she's literally straddling me. Then she hisses out an "Oh fuck."

I try to lift her up because she's now discovered how hard I am. It's morning, and Tessa's panty-clad body is rubbing against me. I couldn't think my way out of a boner right now if I tried. "Tessa," I warn.

Her eyes flash open. "I'm sorry," she murmurs, but she doesn't stop what she's doing. Instead, she rests her hand against my chest, balancing herself, and she rolls her hips again. "Fuck, Ry," she rasps. "I'm trying to stop."

I squeeze my eyes shut. The girl is literally using me to pleasure herself right now.

Her hips swivel again. "Tell me to stop," she says softly, her green eyes still hazy from sleep.

I don't. Instead, I hold her hips and pull her forward, rubbing her against my entire length. A whimper leaves her throat, and I can't help it; I do it again.

"Does that feel good?" I ask.

"So good," she mutters as she shifts back and forth again, her movements clearly stimulating her clit.

"That's it, Pix. Use me to come."

I've said lots of things to my best friend over the years, probably more words than I've said to anyone else, but I never imagined that phrase would come out of my mouth. And yet as soon as I say it, Tessa digs her teeth into her plump bottom lip and mutters, "Oh, thank God," as she chases her orgasm.

Her red hair is messy from sleep, and it sways back and forth as she rides me. The sounds coming out of her mouth are dirty, downright filthy, and I know I'll hear them in my head for the rest of my life. "*Your cock is so fucking big, Ry. Oh fuck, it feels so good against my pussy. I'm dripping for you. Can you feel how wet I am? Fuck, Ry, what are we doing?*"

I can feel her leaking through my sweats, my own orgasm so fucking close I need to think of something else—anything else—because I really don't want to come in my pants.

"Say something, Ry. Tell me it feels good, please."

She looks down at me, vulnerable and turned on at the same time, and so fucking gorgeous.

"You look so pretty riding me, Pix," I admit as I reach up to push back her hair. "Now be a good girl and come all over my cock."

She closes her eyes and leans back, her hair falling behind her shoulders as she hurtles into her orgasm, crying out my name as she comes, and I swear I've never loved a single syllable she's uttered more.

She's breathtaking. Somehow, I keep my composure and focus on her. The way her skin is tinged pink, how little beads of sweat dot her forehead.

She slumps against me and moves her hand down, as if she's trying to get in my pants, but I stop her movement.

"Just rest, Tessa, I'm okay." I kiss her forehead.

She looks up at me, her eyebrows furrowing. "But—"

I press my fingers over her lips. "Please," I beg. I can't let her touch me. Once I feel her hands around my cock, I'll never be able to un-feel it. And this isn't forever. This isn't really anything.

The phone beside my bed rings, and I reach for it, knowing it's the perfect distraction. "It's Sarah," I tell Tessa. "She's just letting me know she and Erin are on their way over."

Tessa nods at me, but the light has left her eyes. She's still thrown from what just happened. Hell, so am I, but I can't focus on that right now.

I answer the phone and slide out of bed, "Hey, sis."

"Hi, we're on our way. You want me to pick up coffee for you and Tessa?"

"Nah, we're okay. I'm going to make a pot now. Tell Erin I'm making Nutella pancakes and bacon."

My niece screeches in the background. "You just told her," Sarah says. "You're on speaker."

I laugh.

"So don't say anything you don't want her to hear," my sister reminds me.

Like how I just let my best friend come on my cock? Yeah, I won't be sharing that bit of information with Sarah or my niece. *Or any-fucking-one*. Especially not Shawn, who will have so many things to say about it.

I turn back to look at Tessa, but she's already sliding out of bed and fumbling through her luggage. Fuck, she looks tense. "Okay, Sarah, I'll see you in a few," I mutter before pressing End. "Tess," I say, waiting for her to stop her movements, but she continues rifling through her luggage. "Tessa," I try again, moving in her direction. When she still doesn't turn around, I grab her elbow and force her to look at me. "Pix, what are you doing?"

Her gaze remains trained on the floor. "I'm so sorry, Ryan."

She never calls me Ryan. *Ever.* I'm Ry, big guy, lumbersnack, apparently, but never just Ryan.

I lift her chin, forcing her to look at me. "There is nothing for you to be sorry for."

She heaves a loud sigh. "I used you to pleasure myself…it's…" she pauses as she tries to look away, but I hold her chin tightly so she can't, "mortifying," she finally finishes.

Clearly my plan of not allowing her to touch me backfired. That she thinks I didn't want her to, or that I didn't enjoy being used for her pleasure, is enough to make me sick. And make me admit the truth. "Tessa, you riding me…using me to get off? Fuck, there is nothing hotter."

"But you didn't want me to touch you…" she says softly.

"No, babe. I can't let you touch me because I won't be able to hold back if you do."

Just like she's never called me Ryan, I've never called her babe. But the second it comes out, it feels right. It also makes something in her eyes flicker, which only makes me feel more possessive over the term. I want her to be that to me. I want it so fucking bad that I can't say it again.

"What if I don't want you to hold back?" she asks softly, a challenging look in her eye.

I shake my head. My sister and niece are going to be here any minute, and I have a boner but absolutely no time to deal with it. I pull Tessa into my arms and hug her instead. "Pix, you don't know what you're asking. But I promise you can use me as much as you want this week."

She softens against me, and her arms round my waist as she pulls me tight. "I'm not using you, Ry." She pulls back and walks to the bathroom, leaving me wondering what the hell she means and if I'm even ready to find out.

I throw on a Lake Tahoe Fire T-shirt and another pair of sweatpants and head to the other bathroom to get cleaned up. When Tessa comes out of my room in a pair of black tights and another one of my oversized flannels, I can't help but smile. There is nothing hotter than the way she looked wearing one with no pants last night. She was all legs and smooth skin. But now she's wearing a big smile, looking like her normal self. Her shyness and mortification over this morning is all but a distant memory. Her hair is still a bit messy, though, and I have to turn away before I get hard again. Seeing her in my shirts all week is going to be a problem. Especially when I think about the way she looked with it falling over her shoulder as she rode my cock.

"Coffee?" I offer, holding out a cup.

"Thanks. What's that I smell? Bacon?" She accepts the cup with a smile.

When she peers into the oven, I take the time to stare at her ass.

She spins around and smiles. "You like what you see, Ry?" she teases.

I shake my head and clear my throat. "I'm making pancakes too. They're Erin's favorite."

Tessa's teasing smile softens, and she reaches out to touch my cheek. "You're a good uncle, aren't you?"

I stare down at her, loving the feel of her hand against my cheek, of her body in my shirt, of her lips so close to mine. But I need her closer. I take the coffee cup out of her hand and place it on the counter, then lift her and set her next to it. I press myself between her legs, push her hair back out of her face and stare down at her. "I like having you here," I admit.

"What are we doing, Ry?" she asks as her hands find my face again and her eyes dart to my lips.

The sound of tires on gravel echoes outside, and I know we're out of time. I lean my forehead against hers and sigh. "Don't know, Pix. How 'bout we don't try to figure it out right now? We've got a relationship to fake anyway, so let's just…" I pause, looking for a way to explain what I'm offering.

"See how it goes?" Tessa supplies.

I hold her attention as I nod. "Yeah, let's see how it goes. Let's not hold back…if something feels…"

"Good?" she provides.

I gulp. "Yeah, if something feels good, let's not apologize for it… let's just…"

Tessa leans in and presses her lips against the side of my mouth. "Do what feels good," she murmurs as tiny feet pound on the deck outside before the door swings open.

"Uncle Ryannn!" Erin screams, "I'm here!" I rub my nose against Tessa's and then spin to face my niece. She has the good grace to look sheepish when she sees us. "Sorry," she mock whispers. "Figured you'd be in the other room."

Erin begins working to take off her gloves, her snow-covered boots, and her jacket, but she leaves her hat on. Her head is always cold, and she doesn't often take off her hat in front of strangers. As excited as she is to officially meet Tessa, I can tell she's still nervous that Tessa will stare. I know she won't though. Tessa knows about my niece's alopecia, and even if she didn't, she's the type of person who always makes others feel comfortable. But Erin has dealt with her fair share of stares and whispers, so we'll have to ease her into this.

"Come on, Pix," I say, tugging on her arm before I lift her off the counter. "Erin has been dying to meet you in person."

My sister comes barreling in the door with snow on her hands and knees.

"What happened to you?" I ask as I head in her direction and hand her a towel I keep by the door for snow-covered boots. I scoop Erin up for a hug, and she wraps her hands around my neck and leans against my shoulder.

"I slipped on the black ice outside," she says, annoyance lacing her words.

"Sorry, I'll go put some salt down." I reach for my own boots and settle Erin back on the carpet.

Sarah puts her hand on my forearm. "It's fine. Do it in a few minutes."

I can feel Tessa behind me, and I spin to find her watching us nervously.

"God, it's been forever since I've seen you, Tessa, but you literally look the same as you did in high school." My sister leans around me and pulls Tessa in for a hug.

"It's good to see you," Tessa says as her smile grows bigger when she turns to Erin. "And you must be the coolest eight-year-old in town. Ry was just telling me he's making us pancakes."

Erin wears a matching smile, looking up at Tessa like she's a shiny new toy. "With Nutella in them?" Erin tests.

I nod. "Yup, wouldn't dare do it any other way," I say as I pull Erin against my hip again.

"Is that a Jojo Siwa bow on your hat?" Tessa asks my niece, and I swear Erin silently squeals.

"You know Jojo Siwa?"

"Um, duh, she was amazing on Dancing with the Stars," Tessa replies. "I actually got to interview her after she won."

"No freaking way!" Erin slips the hat off her head and shows the bow to Tessa.

Sarah shoots me a look and mouths, "That was quick." Tessa doesn't react to my niece's bald head, her eyes instead remaining trained on the bow, and she grabs Erin's hand as they walk into the living room to sit down.

"Yup, I have her manager's cell phone number. Maybe we could get some more bows for you."

"My mom has to sew them onto hats," Erin admits.

Tessa's eyes soften, and she pulls Erin in for a side hug. "Well, I can't sew, so your mom is like a superhero to me. But I bet we could get headbands made with the bows too."

I leave them to their discussion and walk to the kitchen to get to work on the pancakes. Sarah follows closely behind.

"How are things going?" she says in a low voice.

I reach into the fridge to grab the eggs and shrug. "Fine, why?"

"Because she's finally here," Sarah whispers.

I turn back to Tessa and watch as the two women who mean the world to me chat. It stirs something in me, seeing Tessa with Erin. Seeing Tessa in this house was one thing. In my bed, on top of me, it's all starting to mess with my head. But this, seeing Tessa with my family? It feels right.

"Uncle Ryan, can we go downtown today?" Erin asks from the other room. She gets up and walks into the kitchen, inspecting my mixing skills.

"Too lumpy?" I tease.

She smiles a big toothy grin. "Needs more chocolate," she instructs.

Tessa laughs from behind me. It's a husky laugh, and without thought, I turn toward her, taking her hips in my hands and pulling her against me. She leans in and snuggles into my chest.

"Feels good," she murmurs.

I hold her eyes for a moment before I respond. "Does," I admit.

"So town?" Erin says, interrupting us.

Sarah laughs and shakes her head. Yeah, my sister knows I'm having trouble piecing together a sentence with Tessa in my arms. "You guys have a big day," Sarah offers.

"Oh yeah?" Tessa asks.

Sarah laughs and points at her daughter. "Yeah, this one has big plans for you. She's trying to get you to fall in love with Tahoe."

Tessa grins. "That won't be hard. This place, from what little I've seen, is incredible."

"Why are we trying to get Tessa to fall in love?" I ask Erin.

Erin looks at her mother sheepishly and then swings her gaze back to me, gulping down her words.

"Come on, munchkin. Out with it," I say, kneeling down to her level.

Above us, my sister interjects. "She wants Tessa to love it so much she moves here. That way you won't leave."

"Leave?" I ask, confused. I can feel Tessa stiffen next to me.

Erin nods. "You know…since Tessa is your girlfriend, and she lives in Boston."

I inhale a breath, the reality of our situation hitting me again.

Tessa grabs Erin's hand and squeezes. "I am totally down for being convinced, so you better show me all the good spots." She winks at me. "Tell me what you have planned today."

I wish it didn't hurt to see that.

What am I doing giving that kind of false hope to Erin? She has a hard enough time with kids her own age not sticking around—the last thing I need is for her to worry that I'm leaving or believe that Tessa is staying.

My sister, probably sensing the tension, grabs Erin in a hug. "Okay, bug, promise to be good and have fun. I'll see you tonight for the Christmas pageant." She turns to me. "You still okay getting her dressed and bringing her? I left her outfit in the car, but I can always—"

I put up my hand. "I'll grab it for you and put down some salt. Tessa and I would love to take her."

Tessa is already leading Erin to the couch. "How 'bout you tell me about this pageant?"

Chapter 9

TESSA

After we eat breakfast and clean up the kitchen, Ryan gives Erin and me thirty minutes to digest and get bundled up before we start on Erin's wish list for the day. First up is a coffee place she tells me is her mother's favorite—since I'm an adult, she assumes I like coffee.

"You assume right, kid," I tell her as I squeeze her into my side when we walk into the coffee shop. It smells like fudge and cocoa beans and fresh baked goods. I sniff the air, trying to take in every scent and commit them to memory. "This place is amazing," I say in awe.

Erin looks up at Ryan with a sly smile. She's devious, and I freaking love it.

"So what desserts are best here?" I ask her.

"You just had five Nutella pancakes. Where the heck are you going to put more food?" Ryan grabs my waist and asks with a loud sigh.

I shrug. It drives Grace crazy that I can devour sweets without gaining a pound. I should feel bad about it, but I love sugar too much. It's like my one enjoyment in life since sex has been non-existent for the majority of my thirties. Not that I don't have dalliances, but after a while a girl has to hold out and just hang with Buzz Lightyear—my favorite vibrator. It's too hard to continually put myself out there. Honestly, I'm exhausted from dating. I don't know what it is that Ryan and I are doing…but like he said, I'll just go with it because damn, did it feel good this morning.

"We've got plenty of room, right Erin?" I say, moving out of Ryan's grasp so she and I can look at the glass display of desserts.

After we select a croissant, a custard cupcake that looks insanely good, and a blueberry muffin—because its fruit, so clearly its healthy—we sit down with our hot drinks and inhale our food.

"Are a lot of your friends in the pageant tonight?" I ask as I hold my stomach, officially full and in need of a nap.

Erin shrugs, and I feel Ryan's eyes on me. The look he gives me warns me to be careful about bringing it up, but I vividly remember feeling left out. Being belittled. And unfortunately, the culprit was usually the girl he loved, so I couldn't escape it without losing my best friend. What I wanted back then more than anything was for someone to see what I was going through. Someone to see me for me and not just assume that because I was loud, I was fine.

We don't always need to feel accepted, but it is so important to feel heard. To feel seen. Now that I'm older, I get that. But as a young, impressionable girl, it was debilitating not being seen by the one person I held in such high regard. But it wasn't Ryan's fault. He was young too.

Although I know no one can fix bullying overnight—hell, I'm not sure it can ever be fixed completely, some people are just genuinely mean—I do think having people in your life to remind you that you matter is key.

I may not know Erin that well, but I can tell she needs someone to show interest in this, not shy away from the topic.

And I've never been shy.

But she also barely knows me. So I won't push. I'll give her a bit of time to get to know me and then make sure she knows she can open up.

"So where to next?" I say, an upbeat smile on my face.

Erin brightens. "Now you get to meet Uncle Ryan's brothers."

My brows knit together. Ryan doesn't have brothers.

Ryan squeezes my leg. "We going to the fire station, Erin?"

She nods.

Oh, hot firemen. Maybe I can convince Ryan to put on his gear and have one of the guys watch Erin while we take a ride down his pole.

Okay, even I rolled my eyes at that one. As Grace likes to say, I'm ridiculous.

We get refills of our drinks—hot chocolate for Erin, coffee for Ryan, and a mix of the two for me—and we're off to face the cold again.

As it is officially early afternoon on Christmas Eve, the streets are getting busier, likely people getting out of work early and doing last-minute shopping. There is an excitement in the air, an anticipation of what's to come, and it's also just really freaking cold.

"Whoa, is that a horse and carriage?" I ask as I point to one heading down the road.

Erin nods up at me with a twinkle in her eye. If I believed it was possible, I would think she actually hired the carriage driver to make the entire area seem more magical. It's adorable how concerned she is with making me fall in love with this place. Truth is, she doesn't have to work hard. I'm liking it more by the minute.

Ryan walks on the side closest to the road, and Erin swings her hands between us as we stroll down the sidewalk. Snow is glistening against the buildings and caking the trees, but the street and sidewalks remain clear. It's nothing like Boston, which can be a disaster when it snows. All the cars and the tight streets make it hard to keep up when we get a lot of snow.

Normally, I just stay home on snow days. I curl up with a good book or pull out my computer to type up a story of my own. I started writing for myself a few years ago. Short, steamy novellas that are quick and dirty with a lot of heart. I'd never actually consider publishing them, but I enjoy writing them. It's something just for me. Not even Grace knows about their existence.

I'm currently working on a friends-to-lovers book, and I was just getting to the spicy part the other night. Maybe I'll take another stab at it while I'm here. Lord knows I have enough thoughts running through my brain to write several spicy scenes.

I risk a glance in Ryan's direction, and my heart does a stupid little flutter thing when he winks at me over Erin's head. I bite the inside of my cheek to convince myself that this is real—that my best friend is actually looking at me like he is. Because right now, I swear he's thinking about all the same filthy things. Then again, he pointed out how we need to fake this relationship, so maybe he's just really good at acting.

I shake my head of all the thoughts and look up to see the red brick fire station and a fire truck looming before us. I laugh when we walk by it. It doesn't look nearly so big with Ryan beside it. He's like this giant of a man, with his long hair slipping out of his man bun under his hat and his broad chest. I have to clench my thighs when I imagine sitting atop the truck while Ryan goes to town, railing me.

So much for removing filthy thoughts from my head. This is getting out of control.

"Ry, what are you doing here? I thought the hot girl was visiting you," a man says as he jumps down from the truck wearing a blue T-shirt and fireman overalls. He's got black smudges all over his hands and arms, leaving him looking dirty and delicious. I store away the description so I can use it for a novella in the future.

Also, hot girl. Does Ryan think about me that way? Or is it just something he said because he's supposed to be fake dating me? God, this is getting complicated.

Ryan turns to me, and I see a slight flush to his cheeks. Is he embarrassed? I freaking rode him like a toy horse this morning, and *he's* embarrassed? *I can't.*

"This is Tessa. Tessa this is Deek," Ryan says as he points to his friend.

The man holds out his grimy hand and then grimaces before pulling it back and wiping it on his coveralls. "Sorry." He laughs and looks down at Erin. "Now what is our favorite eight-year-old doing with Uncle Ryan today? You excited for Christmas, kid?"

Erin nods. "Yup. I already talked to Santa and asked him for my gift and everything."

I let out a soft laugh, her innocence taking me by surprise. I'm never around kids.

"And Ryan told me you're in the Christmas pageant tonight. Are you excited?"

She gets a bit shier with the mention of the pageant, and my insides buckle. I hate seeing her insecure. I'm not the type of person to watch someone struggle. I need to do something. Somehow. But I'm never around kids, and I don't know what I can do. So instead, I just reach out my hand to her and allow her to show us around a place where she's clearly comfortable.

As Ryan introduces me to the rest of the guys, they all make comments or give knowing looks like Deek did about who I am. As we walk back to the bunk room so he can show me where they sleep, I nudge him with my elbow. "So, you've mentioned me a time or two, huh?"

Ryan laughs as he whispers in my ear, "Yeah, Pix. You happen to be my favorite person. I guess I talk about you a bit."

I'm thrown off kilter by his admission. It's not that I didn't know it. And God the same is true for him; it's just he says it in a way I don't think he would have last week. It has more meaning. I'm just trying to figure out what it is.

He continues, almost as if he can sense my questioning. "And since we talk every night…I can't hide it from the guys I work twenty-four-hour shifts with."

Makes more sense. I nod and turn away from him, flushed and unsure of what this feeling in my chest is. It's getting tighter, and I almost feel like I can't breathe. His words have literally stolen the breath from me.

But once again, Ryan knows what to do. He reaches down and grabs my hand. "It feels good to tell you how I feel. Is that okay?" He meets my eyes and squeezes my hand.

I look at our connection. It does feel good. Being with him. Touching him. Sharing our truths.

"Always, Ry. I always want your truths."

His lips slowly turn up, morphing into a sexy grin. God, how did I not notice this side of Ryan? Or maybe this is how he acts when he's in a relationship…like the one we're portraying. The fake one.

I ignore that thought as we continue staring at one another like two freaking teenagers, our grins matching and our eyes sparkling with promise. But my attention is stolen when Erin hurls herself onto a bed and bounces up and down. "This is Uncle Ryan's bed!"

Ryan squeezes my hand one last time, then lets go. When he does, I have to grab hold of it with my other hand to keep myself from reaching out for him. Ryan runs over and throws himself onto the bed, making Erin bounce and squeal. Then he pulls her on top of him and tickles her. "Hey, don't mess up my sheets, munchkin!"

She squeals, and my heart clenches again. *What is happening to me? And do I want it to stop?*

Chapter 10

RYAN

Erin gets quieter as the daylight disappears and the stars descend on the sky. I clench my jaw and scratch my head, trying to figure out a way to calm her down. We've kept her occupied all day, and she had more sugar than she'll ever need, but I can still feel her shutting down before the show. She hates being in front of a crowd because she never knows what their reaction will be to her bald head. But at the same time, she loves to be on stage. When she's not shy, she has a smile that lights up a room, the voice of an angel, and a personality that makes me proud. But people don't always know how to react to her. They don't know if she's sick, if they should feel pity for her, but Erin isn't someone to pity. She's fierce and beautiful, and every day she shows how strong she is. But the constant stares and questions can get tiring.

And don't even get me started on kids. She's been called weird, strange, different…all because she's missing hair. It's infuriating, but I know most just don't *know* any better.

I walk into the bedroom and find Erin sitting on my bed watching Tessa spin in an emerald-green sweater dress that highlights her creamy, freckle-covered legs. "What about this one?" she asks Erin.

I groan lowly.

Tessa shoots me a flirty smile. "You don't like it, big guy?"

I walk right up to her and press a kiss against her cheek as I squeeze her hip. "You look gorgeous, Pix. What is there not to like?"

Her freckles blend with the rosy color that tinges her cheeks.

"Can I do your hair?" Erin asks as she looks up at Tessa.

Tessa's eyes dart to mine, and I nod. It may seem odd, but my niece loves doing people's hair. "She's pretty good at it," I offer.

Erin crosses her arms and huffs. "Pretty good, Uncle Ry? Everyone loved the braid I did for you last week!"

I laugh.

"A braid?" Tessa teases.

Erin smiles. "Yeah, and to think, he had offered to shave off that hair so we could be twins."

I duck out of Tessa's line of sight, but I can feel her eyes on me.

"But you love your hair," Tessa says quietly as she sits down in front of Erin so she can get to work on her locks.

"I love Erin more," I say easily before walking to the closet to grab my clothes.

I slide the hangers across the rack, searching for a shirt I know is in here somewhere. It takes a few minutes, but I finally locate the green and black checkered shirt and grab a tie to match. Then I find my black slacks and shoes. When I turn around, I stare down at the way Erin is pulling on Tessa's hair while Tessa looks up at her, both of them laughing about something. She's so good with her.

I shake the thought from my head. This is temporary. She's here for a few days. *Enjoy it. Let it all feel good and don't get too attached.* But as I walk out of the room and hear Erin giggle loudly again—so free, so happy, and no longer nervous about the pageant—I know I'm already too far gone.

When I walk back into the room, Erin has done a braid through the side of Tessa's hair, leaving the rest of it wild and free. She looks so damn pretty. But it's the way she's kneeling in front of Erin and talking quietly that has me paused at the door.

"Here, I have something for you," Tessa says as she reaches behind her and pulls out a red gift bag with gold foil sticking out of it. *Where did she get that?*

"You bought me a present?" Erin asks, her voice saccharine, and her eyes welling with happy tears.

Tessa shrugs like it's no big deal. "Saw something while we were in town. Every angel needs a halo," she says as she watches Erin open the package.

Erin sucks in a breath when she pulls out a soft halo covered with white feathers which glitters and sparkles as Erin spins it in her hand. She looks at Tessa like she hung the moon. "Will you help me put it on?"

Tessa smiles and places her on the bed while she adjusts the halo on her head. With Erin's gold dress, the halo on her head, and a tiny bit of Tessa's lip gloss, Erin lights up the entire room.

"You look beautiful," Tessa says as she swipes a little blush onto Erin's cheeks.

She reaches up to Tessa's hand and holds her still. "You think I'm beautiful?"

Tessa falters as she stares down at my niece. I hold my breath as she places the compact on the bed. "Of course I do. Isn't she beautiful, Ry?" Tessa says, looking over and summoning me into the room.

"The most gorgeous girl I've ever seen," I reply as I look at Erin and wink.

"He has to say that. He's my uncle."

Tessa shakes her head. "Your uncle was also the first boy to ever tell me I was beautiful. He doesn't just say things. But you want to know something more important than that?"

Erin nods, and I find myself nodding too.

"He's the first person to ever make me *feel* beautiful. And that's not about my looks, Erin. It's about what's in here," she says, pointing to my niece's heart.

Erin's eyes crinkle as she smiles.

"You are beautiful without this makeup, this dress, and this crown… but let me tell you a little secret." She leans closer as Erin eats up her every word. "Every once in a while, it's okay to put on a crown if you need a little confidence. Even if its invisible. And sometimes it's okay to wear a real one. So chin up buttercup, because you and I are wearing our crowns tonight."

With that, Tessa reaches into the bag, revealing a smaller crown pin. "Can you help me put this on?"

I love her.

In this moment, I know that I love my best friend. Not as a best friend. Not as someone I want to date. My love for her is all-consuming. She's my every thought, the finisher of my sentences, the keeper of my truths, and the only person I'd ever trust to treat my niece so perfectly.

I'm in love with her, and I am so screwed.

Chapter 11

TESSA

As we arrive at the pageant and one of the kids points at Erin, Ryan tenses beside me. "Oh, Erin, where did you get that?" she asks, pointing at the halo.

Erin beams and points to me. "My uncle's girlfriend got it for me. Isn't she pretty?" she asks her friend.

The girl nods and then screeches about someone wearing the same dress, and they set off in another direction. Erin swings her head back before she leaves though. "Thank you, Tessa."

I wink at her and push my hand forward to indicate she should go. Before Ryan and I can have a moment alone, I hear voices calling his name. Ryan turns and whispers in my ear, "I'm sorry."

When we turn, we're met by both of his sisters, their dates, and a woman I instantly recognize as Ryan's mom.

"Mrs. Manning," I say, reaching out to her first, "it's so good to see you."

She squeezes me tightly. "Tessa Sanderson, I cannot believe we got you here for Christmas." Then in a lower voice she says, "I know it certainly is a Christmas miracle for Ryan."

I laugh softly and shake my head. "I'm so happy to be here." I turn to Sarah and hug her next. "Erin was a literal doll today. You're raising one amazing little girl."

Sarah grins. "Thanks, she wasn't too much trouble getting dressed? I know she was stressed, and I feel bad. I had to keep the shop open later today so people could pick up their Christmas arrangements."

Sarah owns a flower shop, so it's understandable that she was busy today. Ryan clears his throat. "It was fine. Actually, Tessa kept Erin pretty calm all day."

Ryan's other sister, Liz, finally reaches in for her hug. "I'm so glad you're here for the wedding. I was convinced Ryan was pulling all our legs when he said you guys were finally giving this a go." Next to her, a woman with long dark hair rolls her eyes. I'm assuming this is her fiancée.

"Liz, can you not throw your poor brother under the bus? I'm sure he doesn't want Tessa to know how much he talks about her."

I laugh as Ryan groans. "You must be Kyra. It's so nice to meet you. Thank you for including me in your wedding."

Both women beam at each other as if they're in on a secret. I guess that's what being in love is, though. You have your own language, your own secrets, your own truths. I turn to Ryan, and he smirks. And in that moment, I feel like we have our own secrets too.

And we do.

We aren't actually dating. We are...I don't even know what the hell we're doing.

But my best friend, the guy who knows everything about me, pulls me into his side and mumbles an admission as we walk into the auditorium. "Feels good having someone by my side at one of these things."

For so long, I've lived alone. I'm thirty-six, and before Grace moved back to the city after her divorce, it really was a lonely existence. And once her baby is here, I'll be alone again. Or I guess she and her child will be my family. But it's nice having all of these people around. All these people who so obviously care about Ryan and, in extension, are welcoming me into the fold without hesitation.

I lean into his arm and say honestly, "It feels good to be a part of these things."

WISHING FOR CHAMPAGNE KISSES

We stare at one another for a moment before sliding in to the row of seats. It feels like things are changing. Like there is a real possibility here. And for once in my life, I want to plan things. I want to know where this is going. I don't want to just live for the night. I want more.

"You sure you're comfortable staying here?" Ryan asks as we walk through the door of Sarah's house. Apparently this has been a family tradition since Erin was born. Everyone sleeps here so they all wake up together on Christmas morning.

"I'm thrilled. Seriously, Ry, pretend I'm not here and just do what you normally do. This is your family holiday." I follow him over the threshold, but before I can walk a step farther, he pushes me back against the wall. A squeak sounds from my throat as I look up into his eyes.

"You make it impossible to pretend you're not here, Tessa. You have to know…you're my family, too." He moves a hand to my cheek and rubs his thumb softly against my skin.

Even though I want to sink into the feeling of him against me, I keep my eyes trained on him.

"I'm so happy you're here," he whispers.

I want to kiss him. In this moment, I want my lips on his so badly I can practically feel my feet lifting as I try to get closer, but he's so tall, and I'm so short. And then I hear Erin's laughter, and when I look around Ryan to find the little girl smiling at both of us, I maneuver under his arms and scoop her up. Clearly, it's not time for our first kiss.

And honestly…for once, I'm not trying to rush it. I'm okay with taking things at a slower pace with Ryan. We've waited decades. What's a few more hours or days? Eventually I'll feel those lips against mine, and I'm pretty sure I'll need to build up some courage before then. This feeling inside me is real, and I'm nervous about what it all means.

I really hope he feels the same and he's not just going along with it because I threw myself at him this morning. Until I know that for sure, I need to guard my heart and my lips.

"You guys have the guest bedroom. Liz and Kyra offered to bunk with Erin tonight in the basement, and Mom took Erin's room," Sarah says.

"Oh, we can take the basement," I say.

Ryan laughs. "Yeah, no. Don't offer that."

Liz walks up the stairs and shakes her head. "Yeah, I'm not the greatest sister, but even I won't do that to Ryan."

I look around, confused. "Am I missing something?"

"Just that your boyfriend is six foot three and over two hundred and thirty pounds," Liz says not so gently.

I laugh as Ryan recoils. "Hey."

"He wouldn't last on a pull-out couch. Perks of dating a big guy, I guess," she says to me with a wink.

Kyra walks in and smiles at Liz. "Oh, feel free to date whatever man you want," she teases.

Liz leans against her fiancée. "Yeah, I'm good with you, but thanks."

It's so warm in here. Not hot. But warm as in lovely—I watch as they all verbally poke and prod at each other with a gentle happiness. Ryan is smiling, Liz and Kyra are cuddled up, and Sarah leans down and presses a kiss against Erin's cheek.

"Bill went to get Mom from her house, so why don't you guys go get settled in your room, then we can play Jenga."

Erin rubs her hands together. "Uncle Ryan, you still gonna be on my team?"

He offers her a fist bump. "Always, munchkin."

My insides squeeze together seeing this big, man-bun wearing guy tower over his niece and melt for her.

He turns back to me. "Come on, Pix, we gotta get game ready." He winks at me before throwing me over his shoulder and grabbing both our bags.

I laugh the entire way to the room.

When he places my feet on the ground, I smack him on the arm. "Ryan Manning, you can't just pick people up and run around with them."

He laughs. "I mean, it's kind of my job."

He does have a point. I guess firefighters do that sometimes. "Fine, but not this person." I point to my chest and stare up at him, pretending to be annoyed.

He shakes his head and puts our bags down on the queen-size bed. It's covered with a bright red blanket featuring a Christmas tree so gaudy it looks like Clark Griswold threw up.

He turns back and pushes me against the door. "Now I think we were in the middle of something before…" he says softly as his gaze settles on me. Minor hesitation flashes in his eyes as he waits for me to react.

"And what was that?" I tease as my lips pull upward and I inch up higher on my toes, pulling on his neck so he's moving closer to me. "Was it a discussion about how abnormally large you are?"

He shakes his head, the smile reaching his eyes as he inches a tiny bit closer. "No. Maybe it was how abnormally small you are?" he questions.

I shake my head as I pull on the arm he's using to cage me in. I put it on my ass so it gives me a little support while I climb him. "Pretty sure that wasn't it either," I reply as I wrap my legs around his waist and he hoists me closer so we're nose to nose.

He brushes his nose against mine and lets out a soft exhale. "I need to kiss you, Pix…I *really* need to kiss you."

With those words, I'm confident this isn't just about the fake dating. I'm so ready to finally feel his lips against mine. I've been waiting decades for this.

Decades.

Without thinking, I beg. "Please." My voice comes out as a rasp, a literal gasp for air because that's what I imagine a kiss from Ryan will feel like. I'm gasping for him. For years I've been floating above him. He's the one who's buoyed me. But right now, the knowledge that he could pull away, that I'll never have a taste of perfection, is drowning me.

Ryan shudders, and I say it again. "Please, Ryan. Kiss me."

His eyes soften as his hand tightens on my waist. His fingers dig into my hip as he pulls me even closer. "Are you sure you want this?" he asks as if he isn't holding me in place. As if he would possibly let me say no. His grasp on me is so firm I know there will be a bruise tomorrow.

I smile—I want all of his marks—and tip my head back, offering him my mouth, and beg, "Do it."

Ryan presses his lips softly against mine, dusting them with little kisses. I squeeze him tighter between my thighs as I get just a taste of him. Aftershave, a hint of wood, maybe a little bit of fire, and a hell of a lot of pheromones. Unable to help myself, I nip at his bottom lip, pulling it into mine.

"Fuck, Pix…" He groans.

"So good," I murmur back as I slip my tongue into his mouth, and I finally get all of him to myself.

He grips my ass tighter with one hand and uses the other one to hold us against the wall. I grip his back, pushing my hips into his, seeking everything in this moment. Our lips tangle, our breaths mingle together, and I'm left panting as he pulls away. I try to bite his lip, to keep him in place, but he laughs huskily and pushes us off the wall and sits on the bed.

I'm straddling him and so ready to continue what we're doing. I lean in for another kiss, but he stops me.

"Tess…if we don't stop this, I'm going to fuck you against that door with my family on the other side of the wall…and I just *can't*."

My pussy flutters to life with the way he talks. I've never heard Ryan speak like that, and *God*…there is just something about my sweet Ryan losing his senses because of me.

I shift on his lap, rubbing myself against him, and bite at his chin.

"Tessa, *fuck…*" He groans as he grabs my head and pulls my lips back to his. His kiss is demanding, controlling. It's the opposite of what I imagined this would be like. He rubs me against him, controlling my hip movement, and then licks up my neck before pushing me back and staring at me. "You, Tessa Sanderson, are my teenage fantasy come to life."

I laugh, because even if he's re-writing history, I like his version better, and he gives me one of his soft grins. There's my Ry.

He groans again when I circle his very obvious erection, the head of it hitting me precisely where I need the attention. "I'm not kidding, Pix…I want you so bad, but we—"

I take his lip between my teeth and leave my eyes on him. "Shh. I know, big guy. Just getting a little taste." I wrap my arms around him, and he drops his forehead to my chest. "We have plenty of time for all of this," I remind him.

Ryan lifts his head and stares at me, his brown eyes molten and hungry. "Don't think I'll ever get enough."

"Truth?" I ask.

He nods, his eyes locked with mine.

"Neither do I," I reply before taking his cheeks in my hand and pressing a soft kiss against his lips. "We're good, Ry. I promise."

He squeezes me tight and then sets me on my feet.

"Now tell me what I need to do to beat your family in Jenga," I toss back as I dig into my bag in search of clothes.

Chapter 12

RYAN

Tessa and Erin's tiny hands make us a shoo-in to win Jenga, and after lots of laughs when Kyra knocks it on top of me as I'm wiggling my fingers in her direction to distract her, Erin and I end up on the floor cuddling while Tessa is in the chair behind us, curled up with a journal.

"What you doing?" Erin asks as she lifts up from her spot on the floor with me and settles herself on the edge of Tessa's chair.

Tessa closes her book but uses her finger to hold her place. "Just writing."

"You're a writer?" Erin asks, intrigue lacing her words.

Tessa nods. "Normally for a magazine and the news," she explains. "But I also like to write for just me."

"What kinds of things?"

Tessa looks at me and then back to Erin, likely trying to decide what to tell her. I'd like to know what she's writing as well.

"Um—just journaling," Tessa stutters, dropping her eyes to her lap.

The light in Erin's eyes dims. "Oh, okay. I'll leave you alone."

Tessa grabs her before she can move. "No, pumpkin. I just…it's just…I like to write short stories for adults." She shoots me a look, her eyebrows raised.

Adult books? Like sexual books? I'm intrigued.

Before my mind can go down that route and give me a boner in front of my niece, Erin interrupts. "Oh, I love books!"

Tessa smiles. "That's good. I always loved reading as a kid. I still do."

"Do you think we could write a story together?" Erin asks.

Tessa opens the book and pushes past a few pages, then looks up eagerly at Erin. "Whatchya want to write about?"

I lean back against the chair, warmed by the fire, while the two of them plot a story…and I gotta be honest—this is the best Christmas Eve yet.

On Christmas morning, I wake up with Tessa snuggled against my chest. Erin and Tessa stayed up until they got four pages of their children's story done. It's a book about a little girl with alopecia whose aunt gives her a crown loaded with superpowers. Tessa met my eyes and smiled at me softly several times as Erin made her write the words.

After Sarah took Erin to bed, we said good night to everyone and settled into the guest room. I was nervous it was going to get out of control again between us, but not because I don't want to take things further. I would rather do it when we're back at my cabin—not in a house full of my relatives. But Tessa just curled up next to me, gave me soft kisses, and then said goodnight. I almost changed my mind and begged her to use me again. I could figure out a way to keep her quiet. But she was sound asleep before I got up the courage to ask.

"Merry Christmas, big guy," Tessa says as she leans on my chest, her hands folded together as she looks up at me.

"Merry Christmas. You sleep okay?"

Her black lashes fan her cheeks as she flutters them dramatically. "With you as a pillow? Slept like a rock."

I squeeze her and pull her closer. "You sure you're okay doing the whole family thing today? We can head back to the cabin later if you want."

She shakes her head. "No, you normally spend Christmas Eve and

Christmas Day with your family, so that's what we're doing," she says before climbing on top of me, her creamy skin coming into view as she straddles me in her tiny shorts.

My hands immediately find her thighs. "Remember what I told you about morning wood?"

She rubs against me. "No, I remember what you showed me."

"Fuck, Tess, don't do that," I warn as she continues moving back and forth.

She leans back, riding me like yesterday. Her tank top is loose, and with her movements, one strap falls over her shoulder. Suddenly, her heavy breast is exposed, her pink nipple growing harder under my gaze.

Fuck it. I reach my hand up to pinch it, and she groans in pleasure. "You like that, Pix?"

She nods, her lips falling open slightly as she moans softly.

"Can you be quiet?"

She looks at me, and God, the things I want to do to her mouth. Instead, I flip her over and hand her the pillow. "Bite down, pretty girl."

I skate my mouth against her breast first, taking her nipple between my teeth as I bite down slightly. She whimpers softly into the pillow as she shifts her hips against me. Fuck, I want to hear her. I wish we could be doing this at the cabin. I wish I could hear her screams, but I need to taste her. I can't wait any longer. I keep my mouth on one nipple and my hand on the other, alternating every so often while she continues to thrash against me and moan.

"Next time we do this, I intend to get you off just by playing with these," I say with one between my teeth and the other in my hand.

Her eyes plead with me to move lower though.

"Please, Ry. I need your mouth."

It's so hot having her ask for what she wants. Tessa is always the person that everyone goes to. She champions everyone, spoils everyone. Right now, I'm going to make her come on my face and leave her so spent she can't do anything but sit on the couch and let me take care of her all day.

"Remember, Pix, the pillow…" I warn, then slide my tongue over her ribs and down her stomach before nibbling softly on her pelvis. I inhale, the sweet scent of her desire infiltrating me as I memorize everything about this moment. I've never wanted a woman like I want Tessa. I think it's because I've wanted her my entire life.

I wish she'd been my first. I wish I hadn't been such a shit and had just had balls back then to make a move on my best friend. Because then I'd have had this a hell of a lot sooner. But even as I say it, I know she wasn't ready. If she's even ready now.

Fuck, I'm not thinking about that.

I bite at her hip again and then lean back so I can slide her now damp shorts and panties off. I throw them somewhere in the corner and stare down at her bare pussy. Her soft, creamy skin glistens. She is so ready for me.

I push her legs a bit wider and settle between her thighs. Then I run my tongue straight up her seam, licking up the mess she made while trying to get relief as I sucked on her nipples. "Such a pretty pussy, Tessa. How come you've been keeping this from me?" I tease between soft licks and kisses against her clit.

She bucks every time I change it up, not knowing what to expect. Her whimpers are lost to the pillow. I hear a soft *please* though, and I lift up a bit and tip the pillow so I can see her.

"You won't keep it from me again, right?"

She shakes her head. "Please, Ry."

"Good girl," I say before moving back down to press my tongue flat against her clit. "Does this feel good?"

She wraps her thighs around my neck and squeezes lightly. "Less talking, Ry…fucking suck."

I chuckle against her skin, and she smiles at me. Even when we're like this…doing something we've never done…we're still us. She's still bossy and funny as fuck, and I'm still lapping up her every word, her every taste, anything she'll give me.

She pulls on my ponytail as she moves my head just like she likes it, and I let her. I get it. As a man, there is nothing hotter than pulling a girl's hair while she sucks my cock, so I'll let her live that fantasy. Fuck, I even enjoy the way it feels when her control slips and her hands lose their grip as my tongue darts in and out of her.

She digs her fingers into my shoulder and starts to shudder, and that's my cue. I stick one finger inside her, and she grabs the pillow and screams into it. I curve my finger as I continue to push in and out, coating her with her own wetness, all while swirling my tongue around her clit. Then finally I take the soft bundle between my lips and squeeze down. She fucking explodes then, her hips rocking as her legs pull me tighter into her until she's literally fucking my face.

I continue to lick even after she's stopped moving and her grip has all but fallen from my shoulders and my hair. With one more press of my lips against her skin, I climb up to the pillow and pull her against my chest.

"Merry Christmas, Pix," I whisper as I press a kiss to her forehead. "Now go back to sleep for a bit."

Chapter 13

TESSA

Who knew Ryan Manning would be so good with his tongue? Even after he's gotten up to grab us coffee, I'm still lying in bed, completely spent. "You have ten minutes," Ryan warns before he heads out of the bedroom with a sly grin on his face. "The munchkin normally wakes up around eight."

I look over at the clock and confirm that it is, in fact, eight a.m. At home I sleep late on Christmas morning. Usually, I'm out at some swanky event on Christmas Eve since my parents live in Florida and I rarely get time off work to visit them. This year, I would have spent Christmas with them, but they had a cruise booked. And as an only child of two only children, I never had any cousins to play with on Christmas morning. I'm just not used to this big-family, white-Christmas kind of thing, and although I've never yearned for it, I did enjoy joining Ryan's family on Christmas Eve when we were kids. Until he started dating Rebecca, that is.

But that's old news. Nothing I should be thinking about anymore. I should probably thank her, since Ryan is so good with his tongue. And instead of stressing about all the years I've missed out on this type of Christmas, I'm just going to enjoy it.

The phone rings beside the bed, and I grab for it quickly, knowing it will be Grace. "Hi, G! How are you and my little alien doing?"

She laughs into the phone. "Merry Christmas, T. Baby is fine. I'm good. Just opened some presents with Cash's family, and now he's spending some time with his grandfather, so figured I'd give you a call. How's Tahoe?"

I lean my head back and smile. "It's really good," I admit. "Like *really* freaking good."

Grace hums an agreement into the phone. "And Ryan? How's he doing?"

I laugh. "He's really freaking good too…with his tongue," I tease.

She laughs loudly and says, "I knew it!"

"Whatever. You're a matchmaker. You should know these things."

Grace hums again. "So, have you guys talked about what this means?"

"No. He legit just left the bed after giving me one of the most intense orgasms of my life while I tried to remain silent…"

She giggles again. "Okay…just…be careful with him. He has real feelings for you, T."

I sigh. "Do you really think so? I mean…I don't know. I think maybe you're right, and I think I have real feelings for him too."

And I don't know what that means.

"The distance…" she starts, and I wait for her to point out the obvious, but instead, she says, "is manageable. I mean, you don't have to be in an office. Most of your work is done by phone or by flying to meet with your interview suspects."

"They're called interview subjects, Grace."

She laughs again. "I'm just teasing."

"You sound happy," I tell her, relieved after everything she's been through.

"I am…and for the record, Tess, you sound happy, too. I know you and I always say that a woman should never put a man before her career…but we also shouldn't put our careers before the right man. We can have it all. We just have to figure out a way to do that."

I hear her and I totally agree. And honestly, I already have an idea in my head. Hopefully it's not too much or too soon for Ryan. Hopefully,

WISHING FOR CHAMPAGNE KISSES

I'm not too much.

"Thanks for calling, Grace. I'll see you next week. Love you."

"Love you, T. Merry Christmas."

Chapter 14

RYAN

Tessa sits curled up on the couch while Erin smiles and shouts about every gift she opens. Being the only child in our family, she's spoiled rotten, but she deserves it because she's the greatest kid I know. She makes sure to include Tessa in her excitement, showing her the new doll my sister got her, the Gameboy I splurged on, and the art supplies we all over-purchased. Erin has an eye for art, and I love seeing her with her tongue sticking out of her mouth as she focuses on her next drawing.

She and Tessa whisper to one another, and I shake my head as I stare at them over my coffee.

"What're you two talking about over there? You better not be plotting to cut my hair or something crazy."

Tessa puts her hand over her chest in mock offense. "I would never touch that hair…I happen to be a big fan." She winks at me, and I have to look away as a smile consumes my face.

"Yeah, Uncle Ryan, we love your hair!"

I laugh because my niece has no idea how much Tessa loves my hair or why.

Sarah settles next to me on the couch. "Erin has really fallen for her," she says softly.

"I understand the feeling," I mumble and take another sip of my coffee.

"So you gonna tell her?"

"Tell her what?"

"How you really feel? How you've always felt? Why you broke up with Rebecca?" she asks just above a whisper.

I glare at her. "What would be the point of that? We're happy, but she's going back to Boston…" I look at Tessa, who is now setting up the art supplies with Erin. She has her journal in her hand again. What is she doing now?

"Because you guys can make this work…you *should* make it work. I haven't seen you this—" I put my hand over my sister's.

"Sarah, I appreciate your concern…and thoughts, I really do, but I'm fine. Things are new with Tessa. Let me explore that without it turning into a thing right now. We have another week to see how it goes. Let us enjoy it."

She gives me a forced smile. "Right. I'm sorry…it's just…I'm with Erin. I don't want you to move."

I laugh. "No one is moving anywhere…"

"So, you're really willing to give her up after this week?" she asks with a raised brow.

And fuck, does that hurt. Because no, I'm not. But I don't have any expectation that she'll stay.

A children's book. That's what Tessa and Erin were setting up earlier. Now that they have the story plotted, Tessa is working on the words while Erin does the drawings. They're so lost in their own world that we don't bother them when we get to work on making lunch—manicotti rolled by hand and meatballs.

But after an hour, Tessa comes to look for me, and she squeals when she sees what we're doing. "Oh, a man in an apron! Yummy!" she teases as she wraps her arms around my waist, squeezing me tight.

She looks up at me with her green eyes so wide and happy that I can't help it. I lean down and drop a kiss on her lips in front of everyone.

She brushes her nose against my cheek when I pull back and whisper, "Feels good."

"Does," I reply. "Now go grab me a napkin so I can actually touch you without making a mess." I hold out my hands to her, which are covered in meat, and she backs away laughing.

"Oh, Mrs. Manning, I've missed your manicotti and meatballs! I'm so excited! How can I help?"

My mom smiles. "First, you can stop with that Mrs. Manning nonsense and just call me…"

My mom pauses for a moment, and I really hope she's not going to say what she's said to every one of my siblings' other halves.

"*Mom*." And there it is.

I expect Tessa to back up or even shoot me a look. But she just smiles and says, "Okay, Mom. Put me to work." And then she's in the kitchen with my family—my sisters and Kyra crowding her and asking questions while my mother teaches her how to roll the pasta.

As if she suddenly realizes I'm still just staring like a creep, and have been for a good two minutes, she looks up and smiles at me. "Come on, Ry, don't leave me hanging. I need your hands to help me."

And those words totally fuck with me. Because she needs my hands, and I need my hands inside her, but that's not what we're talking about right now. So I clear my throat and point to the sink. "Just gonna go get cleaned up, and then I'll be over to help."

She stares at me for another minute, and I feel like everyone is watching us. Her lips fold over themselves as if she's trying to contain her happiness—as if just looking at me makes her grin so wide that she's embarrassed. It leaves me wanting to rake my hands through my hair as I contemplate a way to really make this all work.

But meat…it's on my hands…so I just gulp down my very real feelings and nod at her.

The walk to the sink, which is at most five steps, feels like a million. Because I'm walking away from her. How am I supposed to get close to my best friend, taste her, have her come in my mouth, and then walk away next week? I can't. I—

"So, what is your plan for work, Tessa?" my mom asks, breaking into my thoughts.

I cringe.

"Mom, don't pressure her," I say as I keep my eyes focused, knocking the faucet on with my elbow and then scrubbing my hands clean.

Tessa clears her throat. "Well, I don't really go into the office all that much…" she says softly.

My shoulders stiffen, but I continue to wash my hands long after they're clean in hopes that she'll go on. Finally, her voice fills the silence. "So, really, I can work from anywhere."

I turn the water off as my sisters pepper her with questions.

What does that mean?

Would she really consider moving here?

Could she see herself being happy here?

Who's her next interview?

And I'm sure she's giving them answers to all the questions, but my mind is swirling, wondering if she's just saying this because we're outwardly faking a relationship for the week, or if possibly, just maybe, she would actually consider staying.

After what can only be described as the longest afternoon ever, with so much food that I literally can't wear pants without elastic and a Christmas movie marathon, everyone is dozing in the living room, and I finally have Tessa all to myself.

Over dinner, she held my hand. While we watched movies, she sat on my lap. When we took a break to build snowmen outside, she brought out her and Erin's crown's and then made me take a picture with the two queens. Everything felt right, like we were a real couple, like she was part of the family, like she belonged with me.

But I don't know how to get those words out. How to ask her if what she said was real. If she could actually see herself living here. If her boss would let her commute. If she put real thought into any of this before getting my hopes up. Before getting my family's hopes up. Because if it's just for this fake relationship…God, I get why she said it, and I'm not mad, but fuck, I'd be hurt.

But I'm too scared to ask.

So instead, we cuddle and make out, and she whispers how she can't wait until tomorrow. And all I can think is that it's one day closer to her leaving, so I don't respond. I just hold her tighter.

Chapter 15

TESSA

I'm riding a snow-covered sleigh of emotions today. The past two days were a dream. Ever since arriving in Tahoe, I've felt lighter, happier, more settled than I have for the last few months. The last few years, if I'm honest. Part of that is because Grace is doing better, so my guilt has eased, but it's also because of this place. It's magical. Not because of the snow—or because it reminds me of a Hallmark movie, although it does—but because of the way it makes me feel.

Being with Ryan's family, being included as if I belonged, having his mother tell me to call her Mom and Erin attaching herself to me in that way…all of it feels *right*.

And then there's Ryan. Everything is always right when I'm with him. I don't know why it took me so long to come out here. I think I always knew if I came to visit, I wouldn't want to leave. And I don't. But I'm not worried. I *can* make this work. *I think.*

Beside me, Ryan drives his truck with a grin on his face and my hand in one of his. "Hey, Pix, can I take you on a date today?"

I lean my head back and smile. "Rain check?" I ask.

His brow furrows. "You got plans?"

"Just have to make a few work calls. And unfortunately, it may take a few hours. I haven't checked in since I left."

He nods and his hand loosens on mine.

"I'll make it up to you tonight. I promise."

He just hums an "okay" and delivers me to the house.

When I go to get out of the truck, he stays seated. "You not coming in?"

He fumbles with his keys, which are still in the ignition, and manages to get the house one off it. "Nah, I'm going down to the office for a bit. Catch up on paperwork while you do. You'll be okay, won't you?" he asks, though his voice lacks its normal warmth.

I try to shake away my concern though. It's Ryan. We tell each other everything. If he was upset, or if something was really bothering him, he'd tell me.

"'Kay," I lean in for a kiss. When he doesn't pull away immediately, I bite down on his lip, eliciting a groan from him. I open my eyes slowly and study him, trying to read into his actions and his mood, but he seems fine. "See you in a bit," I say as I take his key and my bag and hop out of the car.

It's only once I get inside that I realize he didn't try to walk me in. With anyone else, it wouldn't mean a thing, but with Ryan, who constantly wants to hold my hand or touch my body to protect me from snow or ice or just life in general…it feels like a bigger deal.

Hours pass, and I'm able to put my concerns over Ryan's mood aside. I'm focused on making everything in my life align. Setting it up so I can have my cake and eat it too. Or my orgasms and my job. More appropriate when we're talking about me.

When the afternoon sunlight disappears and it turns dark, I start to wonder if Ryan got stuck at the fire station. But my calls to his phone go unanswered, and eventually I decide to make myself a sandwich and work on the book Erin and I started. I have a plan for it that I can't wait to show her.

At nine, I settle myself down in bed, but I'm wound up. I haven't heard from Ryan. No replies to my texts…and everything feels like it's slipping out of my fingers. I get back out of bed, pour myself a glass of wine, and pull my favorite toy from my suitcase, knowing I will never fall asleep this riled up.

I don't need a man for an orgasm. I'd just like one. And not just *any* one. I want Ryan.

Fuck. How did I end up in this situation, needy and desperate for a man? I don't care about men. They're toys to me. A means to an end. But Ryan *isn't* any man. He's my Ry. And now we've gone and mucked it all up somehow, and I'm the stressed woman waiting at home for her man.

Is he even my man?

I hate my mind right now. I suddenly understand how desperately insane Grace was all those months ago. But I'm not Grace. I'm not going to cry into a tequila bottle or beg my ex to meet me at a sex club.

I swear she's a lot kinkier than I ever gave her credit for.

No, that's why I have Buzz. And Buzz can take my mind off all of this. A glass of red wine, my vibrator, and an orgasm. That's all I need.

I slip on one of Ryan's flannel shirts, because, okay, maybe I am a little needy. The smell of him will definitely make me come quicker. I'm completely bare under his shirt, which is soft against my nipples and already has me moaning and ready. Then I grab my glass of wine and Buzz, placing them both on the bedside table, before slipping into bed.

Ryan's smell surrounds me. His pillow, his sheets, his comforter, everything in here is him, and I'm already pulled as tight as a thread, ready to snap. I take a sip of wine and start with pulling Ryan's button-up shirt open so the cool air of the room hits my nipples. Immediately, I'm transported to yesterday, when he promised to get me off by touching them alone. As I twist and pull, I wonder how long it would really take.

But just as I'm starting to get myself worked up, I hear a car engine in the distance and listen as the rumbling breaks through the quiet night. The truck idles for a few seconds, and then the quiet is interrupted by the sound of the car door opening and shutting. Boots hit the snow-covered ground and tread up the driveway and to the front door.

I listen, but I'm too turned on to stop my fingers. Instead, I take a sip of wine and spread my legs wider as I grab the butterfly clip from my toy and bring it to the base of my pelvis, but I don't turn it on. There's a remote control next to the toy, and I leave that on the nightstand and wait.

When the door to the bedroom finally creaks open, I know exactly what Ryan is seeing. Me, spread wide on his bed, lit only by the small lamp beside me. His shirt hanging wide open, exposing my breasts. One hand is on my nipple, pulling and tweaking, while the other holds the butterfly against my clit, and I've got a sly grin on my face. "Thought I'd have to do this myself, big boy."

"Fuck, Tess. What are you…" He stops himself as his eyes eat me up, slowly traveling my body. He shakes his head, and his hair, which he doesn't have in a ponytail for once, sways with his movement. My pussy clenches as it begs for the battery-operated toy or Ryan's mouth. Or his cock. Any of the above would do.

"Can ya do me a favor?" I say coyly.

Ryan raises an interested eye.

"See that remote over there?" I say, motioning with my head since my hands are both occupied.

Ryan nods, his jaw taut and his eyes blazing.

"Ya think you could switch it on for me? My hands are a bit full." I smile, and Ryan shakes his head, looking off in the other direction with a smirk on his face before turning back to me.

"You are a fucking dream. And you're going to destroy me."

I nod. "That's my plan, big boy. Now come on over here and help your best friend out. *Please*," I say with a pout.

Ryan undoes his belt buckle, and just the sound of metal clanging against metal sends a pulse between my legs as my body heats. His eyes remain on mine as he lowers his jeans, and then he pulls his Henley over his head. His broad, muscular chest and green boxers make me squirm. "This what you want, Pix?" he says as he sticks his fingers into the hem of his boxers and teases them lower.

Finally, I'm going to see his massive cock.

I. Am. Giddy.

I nod.

"Use your words, Pix. Tell me you want this."

I drip down my leg. "Ry, I don't just want that. I want your cock in my mouth."

Ryan's jaw clenches, and he drops the boxers.

Now I'm not one to fangirl over a penis, but this isn't just any penis. This is my best friend's penis. And ladies, it's something of a masterpiece. It's the kind you want to stare at…and fuck…and lick… and suck…and I'm about to do all those things. "Come here," I say, my voice husky with desire.

Ryan's movements are masculine and slow and sure as he walks toward me, the manhood I'm somewhat obsessed with bobbing as he moves. As he reaches the bed, his eyes darting between my lips, my nipple, which I'm still teasing, and the device I've started moving on my own, he breathes heavily. "Tess, what is that?"

"Oh, this is Buzz's little helper—"

"Who?"

"Buzz," I motion to the side table where my vibrator stands tall. He's such a pretty boy. "He takes me to infinity every time," I say with a smile.

Ryan's laughter fills the room, and I close my eyes in ecstasy. God, I love his laugh.

"You're fucking crazy. You know that, right?" he says as he slides his hand up and down his cock. I can't focus on his words because the way he's gripping himself has me completely lost in desire.

I watch as the head starts to glisten, and I lick my lips. "Please, Ry…"

He looks down at me as he continues to stroke. "You want a taste?"

I meet his eyes and nod.

He looks to the ceiling and then back at me before dropping his knees onto the bed beside me and pressing the tip of his cock against my lips. "Go ahead, Pix. Ruin me." And then he holds my jaw as he slowly feeds his cock into my mouth, leaving me groaning around him.

"Oh fuck, Tess…fuck, that feels so fucking good."

I moan again as I bring my hands to his cock to stroke while I continue to take him in and out of my mouth, licking and sucking as I go, loving all the sounds he makes as I move around him.

He hits the back of my throat on another curse, and then I feel the butterfly on my clit start to suction. My mouth goes slack on a whimper, but I pull him tighter, focusing on how he tastes—salty and sweet—and how he smells like wood-burning fire and smoke, and how he sounds saying my name as he praises me.

"Good girl, Tess. You take my cock like such a fucking good girl." He strokes my hair and my chin and my cheek. "You are so fucking pretty, Pix. I fucking love having you here. Love the way that mouth I'm obsessed with is sucking on me. And your tongue? Fuck, Tess."

He pulls out of my mouth then, and I groan at the loss of contact, but then he settles himself next to me. "I need to taste you too, baby. Sit on me."

I don't hesitate to flip myself over, my ass in his face and my face on his cock.

"I can't tell you how many times I've seen this ass bent over and I've wanted to do this," he says, and runs his fingers from my slit to my ass before smacking lightly.

"Harder," I order.

106

Ryan laughs as he hits me again, and I yelp around his cock. Ryan puts his bearded face between my legs, his scruff burning my sensitive skin, and his tongue darts out to lick my pussy. When he presses his entire tongue inside me as he turns the butterfly back on, I buck in excitement.

"You're dripping onto my face," he says as he licks languidly.

I press into him, riding until I'm screaming out his name. "Ry, I'm gonna come."

"Good girl. Come all over my tongue," he says as I explode.

At the same time, he slides Buzz inside me, turning him on and sending me into another stratosphere. My body pulses around the vibrator, but I don't stop. I suck Ryan's cock, taking him as deep as I can while he moves the vibrator in and out and licks my clit.

"I can't take it," I cry as my orgasm builds again.

Ryan laughs against my skin. "Come on, baby. Give me one more."

I cry out again and squeeze him tighter until his movements are no longer controlled and he's pushing his hips up and fucking my mouth.

"Tess, baby, I'm gonna—" he warns, but I don't let up, and when he finally lets go, his orgasm leaves him groaning out for me. "Oh fuck, Tessa, that feels so fucking good."

I don't stop until he slows down. When he does, I roll off him. Spent and proud.

"Come here, pretty girl," Ryan murmurs as he pulls me up and onto his chest.

I can't help the stupid smile that breaks out across my face when I peek up at him.

"Don't hide that smile, baby. Come here and kiss me."

He lifts me up to meet his mouth. I taste us both, but I don't even care. I am fucking crazy about this guy, and it literally came out of nowhere.

As we pull apart, I feel the need to tell him exactly how I feel. "Truth, Ry?"

He smiles. "Always."

"Everything feels so good."

He laughs. "That it does."

"But earlier…" I start, not wanting to beat around the bush. "You left, and you didn't reply to any of my texts…I just thought…"

Ryan grabs my chin and forces me to look at him. "I had a moment. I'm sorry."

I sigh. "What kind of moment?"

"I'm not like you, Tess. I don't do casual sex. I—"

I push back from him. "Excuse me?" The burn from his words takes me by surprise. Especially when I'm so wrapped up in all my emotions for him.

"Why do you look mad? I'm trying to explain that I had a bit of a freak-out about what we're doing. I know this isn't serious for you, and we said we'd just do what feels good…and obviously everything has felt great, so we just keep pushing the boundaries. But—"

"And you think I wasn't freaking out about our situation because I'm what? A slut? A whore? A woman who's had orgasms from too many different men? Wow…just…fuck, Ry…all this time, that's what you've thought of me?" I hop out of bed, angry, hurt, pissed—really fucking pissed. Destroyed. The man I admire, the one person who was always in my corner, who always had my back, has thought this of me the whole time. I just…I can't.

Ryan's face distorts in pain. "Fuck. No, Tessa, that isn't what I was saying, and that's not what I think."

He reaches out for me, but I push back from the bed and turn away from him, leaning into my suitcase to grab a shirt and pants. I dress quickly and beg my eyes to hold tight to the tears. I cannot cry in front of him.

All this time, he's had the same opinion of me as the rest of them. I guess he did hear Rebecca's murmurs back then.

"Tessa, please turn around," he begs.

I spin around and glare at him. "For the record, Ry, before Carter, I hadn't had sex in two years. This wasn't casual to me. I was ready to upend my whole *life* for you! This was it for me, Ry. The real thing. I had no idea this was just a benefit of having a fake relationship for you. You think I went into this thinking, 'oh, I think I'll just fuck around with my best friend, and then we can go back to normal'? Is that really what you think of me?"

So much for keeping the tears at bay. They pour down my cheeks, and I slump against the bed, completely drained from the gambit of emotions.

Ryan drops to his knees in front of me, grabbing my thighs and staring up at me. "Please, baby, don't cry. Fuck…I fucked this all up."

My shoulders shake as the sobs rack my body. "You really did."

He reaches his hand up to swipe at my tears, but it's pointless. He can't stop them any easier than he can take back what he said. Because that's the power of words. Once they're out, they can't be taken back. The echo of his thoughts in my head won't surrender to his touch.

An alert sounds from his phone, and both our eyes dart to the floor where it rings from his pants. Ryan looks to me and then back to his phone, pure anguish on his face.

"You should get that," I say, lifting myself off the bed and trying to push past him.

Ryan grabs my hips, trying to keep me in place. "Please, Tessa, let's talk this out. This is what we do. We tell each other our truths. We're honest with one another. I was just trying to be honest."

"Your truth hurts," I admit. "My truth was that I'm crazy about you, and yours was that you don't even know me. That all these years, you haven't seen me as the fun, loud girl with insecurities a mile long who's only ever been the real me with one person…*you*. You saw what everyone else sees. You saw the wiseass, the flirt who sleeps around." I shake my head as it settles into my skin. I really thought he knew me. I really thought he saw *me*.

Ryan's face is panicked and pinched together in pain. "No, Tessa—"

The phone blares again.

"You should get that," I say, motioning with my chin to the phone before turning away.

Ryan growls as he reaches to the floor and grabs his phone. "Fuck!" he jeers as he stares down at it. "It's a fucking fire, Tess. I have to go."

I hold myself in place, willing the tears to stop. This is good. He'll leave and I can have a proper breakdown and be back to my normal self before he returns. I nod, trying to keep my voice steady. "Okay."

"Tess," he says as he reaches for me. "I *have* to go. I don't *want* to go." His voice comes out strangled, forcing me to look at him. "You aren't any of those things in my mind. And I'm so fucking sorry."

I nod as another tear skates down my face, and when he closes the door, I drop to the bed and cry.

Chapter 16

TESSA

I haven't heard from Ryan in two days, and it's no secret why. Everyone in town is watching the fires to the south of us. Every fire department in the state has been activated to help. The only saving grace is that rain is coming tonight, and it's supposed to last a few days, so hopefully that will help.

Worry gnaws at me, as do Ryan's words. He needs to be okay. *We* need to be okay. But really, I just need my best friend to get home safe.

Stir crazy with emotion and unable to sit in the room where my heart broke into a million pieces, I head to the bar in hopes of getting an update from the locals.

As soon as I walk into the familiar space, I meet Shawn's eyes across the bar, and he jumps over it and heads in my direction. I crash against his chest as tears stream down my face.

"He's going to be okay," Shawn says firmly as he rubs circles on my back. "Come on, let's get you a drink by the fire and some food."

Exhausted, I shrug. I'm tired of rolling our conversation over in my head. I'm tired of worrying myself sick over whether Ryan is safe. I'm just fucking tired.

He leads me to an oversized chair by the roaring fire, pulls up the ottoman, and gestures for me to relax. "Get cozy. I'll get you an Irish coffee and a menu."

I nod and then call after him, "With whipped cream?"

He smiles, and I feel a small part of myself shift back into place. Just being in the space, Ryan's spot, with his friend, is helping.

Settling on the couch, I take out my phone and stare at it as I try to figure out what I want to say to Ryan. I hate how strained things between us are. I hate that I care but am still so hurt.

Shawn returns with my drink, and I smile as I spot the cherry sitting on the whipped cream. "Thank you."

"He's going to be okay," Shawn says again.

I swallow past the lump lodged in my throat. "I know. He's trained for this, and I have to believe he'll be fine."

Shawn studies me. "But you're still worried."

I shrug and give a small laugh. "Well, yeah. And we kind of got in a fight before he left." I swipe my tongue at the whipped cream and then take a sip of my coffee. The whiskey burns my throat, but it's exactly what I need.

"Really?" Shawn says, as if it's the most preposterous idea.

I laugh again, bitterly this time. "Yeah. Pretty sure it's the only fight we've ever had. I guess that's what I get for kissing my best friend."

Shawn's eyes bulge. "So he finally got his wish."

My stomach somersaults. "His what?"

Shawn smiles and nods toward the bar. "See all those dollars?"

I nod, waiting for him to continue.

"The first night I met Ryan—last New Year's Eve—one of them fell. Normally I don't read them. But when Ryan saw it fall, he asked if I could, so I said I'd read it if he put up his own wish."

"That's what's on those dollars?"

"Yeah. Each of the owners of this bar—there are four of them—was looking for a new start. Their lives had fallen apart, and they decided to open this bar together as their second chance at living a life with their best friends. One of them even found her forever recently." He smiles and shakes his head. "Anyway, they wanted everyone who comes in to be honest about what they'd want in life if they could get a second chance. So the idea is that you write your biggest wish—the one thing you want most—on the dollar, like you're sending out that energy into the universe, and"—he shakes his head again— "I know this sounds crazy, but every time a dollar falls, I think it's a wish coming true."

I laugh, bewildered. "That does sound crazy."

"But it happened again."

"What do you mean?"

"Ryan's wish. It fell. The night you got here." He reaches into his pocket and pulls out his wallet.

"You can't show it to me!" I whisper shout, looking around the room to see if anyone is listening. "That's like reading someone's diary! It's… it's *wrong*."

He laughs. "Ryan is the one who made me start reading them. And clearly you need to see this. Because whatever went wrong, I assure you, the man has been crazy about you since day one. He'll fix it."

I'm not so sure about that. "We're just friends," I say quietly, trying not to let the truth of those words hurt me. For a moment, I thought Ryan was it for me. I let the touches and the kisses and the sweet moments in front of his family convince me that he wanted me for more than just a week of feeling good. But that's all I ever seem to be good for. The laugh, the sex, the night. I'm not the forever girl. I'm the fake girlfriend.

Shawn raises his eyes, clearly calling me on my bullshit. "That could be true, but that's not what Ryan wants."

"Isn't this breaking bro code or something?" I tease as I take another sip of my drink.

"Maybe," he admits. "But honestly, Ryan is the best guy I know."

I nod in agreement. There's nothing to argue about there. I just wish he thought as highly of me.

"Over the last year, I've watched him light up every time he talked to you or about you. So if he did something to screw it up, I think it's important you know that he probably did it with the best of intentions.

Because the guy is crazy about you, and since he can't be here to make you smile, I know he'd want me to."

I blow out a long breath. "Okay, hit me with it," I finally say, deciding that I'll read the damn dollar.

Shawn smirks as he places the dollar bill in my hand.

I wish my best friend was my last first kiss.

I stare at the familiar handwriting in confusion. "Wait, when did you say he wrote this?"

I look up at Shawn and see him smiling at me as he replies, "Last New Year's Eve. He'd just gotten done helping put out a fire, and he looked like shit. But then you called, and he lit up like a fucking firework." Shawn reaches out and touches my hand. "Tessa, the guy's been in love with you since day one. You've gotta see that."

I put down my cup and reach for my purse.

"What are you doing?" Shawn asks.

"I need a dollar!" I almost shout, my pulse racing as I think of what I want. What I've always wanted. How did I get this so wrong? My big dummy wasn't saying I was a floozy. He was trying to tell me he wanted this to be something more, but he's an idiot, so instead, he insulted me. "Also, I need tequila."

"Tequila?" Shawn says, quirking his brow.

"Yes! Tequila. It's how I work things out with my best friend Grace. Bad day? Tequila. Your mother blasts your entire life story on the news? Tequila. Your husband cheats on you? Tequila. Your boyfriend dumps you? Tequila. Your—"

Shawn pats my hand. "I get it. And yeah, I'll grab a bottle."

With the tip of my pen between my teeth, I think about what I want to say. It comes to me almost immediately. I throw down a twenty next to my finished drink, grab my purse and the dollar, and take the tequila bottle that Shawn's holding out to me. "Where you going?" he asks as I give him a quick hug.

"To wait for our best friend to come home."

He smiles. "Thatta girl. Did you think of a wish?"

I nod. "Now let's just hope it comes true."

Chapter 17

RYAN

I'm tired to my bones. The fire is finally under control, so they sent my department home to rest as others arrived as backup. I should sleep at the station. I have no business driving when I'm this tired, but I took a nap on the way back. I just need to get home to Tessa. She needs to know how I feel. She needs to know that I see her. I see all of her, and I want every fucking thing she is. She's it for me. My best friend. My soulmate. My everything. Our pasts don't matter. And knowing I made her think for even a moment that she was anything less than she is? Fuck, do I hate myself for that.

I pull into my driveway, the snow crunching under my tires. My house is completely dark. I can already feel it. She isn't here.

I trudge up the steps anyway, hoping I'm wrong. As I swing the door open and call out her name to an empty house, I know I'm not mistaken. After slipping off my shoes and my jacket, I collapse onto the couch. I'm too late.

"Ry," she shouts as she walks into the house, a bottle of tequila in her hand and a smile on her face. I don't have a second to respond before she's running at me and throwing herself into my arms. "Oh fuck, Ry, I was so worried about you."

My heart hammers in my chest as I take every inch of her in, and my entire body relaxes at the realization that she's not looking at me as if she hates me—as if I've destroyed everything—no, right now she's my best friend again.

I pull her legs around my hips so she's straddling me, then bury my hands in her hair, pulling it out of her face so I can get a good look at her. This is not at all the welcome I expected. "Tess, baby, are you okay?"

She stares at me and then leans in so she's hugging me again, her head on my chest and her arms tight around my neck. "I'm fine, you big dummy. I brought tequila, but I forgot limes." She tries to get up, but I stop her.

"What are you talking about? Why do we need tequila?"

Tessa rolls her eyes. "Because apparently I'm just as bad at this whole love thing as Grace, so we're going to need some tequila to get through this conversation."

I scrub my hands over my face. She's not making any sense. "Talk to me. We don't need tequila to have this conversation."

She gives me a look. "Fine. Truth."

I nod.

"Why did you ask me to be your fake girlfriend?"

I shake my head. I don't know why I'm surprised by her question. She's always direct.

"Because I wanted to see what it was like to be your boyfriend," I admit.

Her forehead wrinkles. "Why?"

"Because I've wanted this since we were kids. I've wanted to hold you on my lap whenever I wanted. I wanted to kiss you, touch you, walk down the street holding hands with you. I wanted to know what it felt like for you to be mine."

She sucks in a breath. "Don't say that. Don't rewrite history. You never made a move. You never said *anything*. You were obsessed with Rebecca, and she broke your heart…it's why you left Boston."

I roll my eyes and squeeze her hips, pulling her closer to me. "For such a smart girl, you really do assume a lot."

"For such a big man, you really are pretty dense," she retorts.

I laugh loudly. "I am. I should have told you ten years ago that *I* broke up with Rebecca. That I only asked her out in high school because you agreed to go to prom with Trent. I should have told you that the reason I left Boston was because I couldn't stand to watch you with other guys. You gave no hint, no indication, that you had any interest in anything more than friendship."

"Wait, you broke up with Rebecca?" she asks, genuinely curious as she stares up at me with her mossy green eyes.

I nod. "I was *in love* with you. Pretty sure I always have been."

She sucks in a breath.

"But it's okay if that's not what you want. Tessa, you're my best friend. The most important person in my life. I can't lose you. If you don't want to do this, if you don't feel the same way, that's fine. Just promise me we can still be friends."

She looks bewildered. Her eyes are wide, and she's shaking her head.

I lean into her so we're nose to nose, crushed. "Please, Tess. I just want to be your best friend again."

"I don't want to be your friend," she says softly. "I don't want to be your fake girlfriend…"

I fight the urge to beg her to change her mind. I close my eyes and hold her tighter. I don't want to let her go.

"Ry, ask me my truth. Ask me why I came. Why I agreed to be your fake girlfriend."

I sigh, nervous to hear her truth. "Why did you come? Why did you agree to be my fake girlfriend?"

"Because I'm not happy. Because when I looked at my life and categorized what made me happy, the first thing on that list was you."

I pull back and search her eyes. I had no idea she was so unhappy.

"Tess," I say, touching her face.

She takes my hand and pulls it against her chest. "You want my biggest truth?" she says as her heart pounds against my hand. "I came because I'm ready for this. Whatever this is. I'm ready to explore it. And that's what we've been doing…but it's not enough now. Dammit, Ry, I wish I had known years ago this was how you felt. That you'd been this unhappy, because if I had known that…" She looks away from me.

"What?" I urge, unable to handle the silence.

"If I had known you were unhappy, then I would have moved mountains to change things."

I lean back against the couch. "You didn't do anything wrong."

She presses closer and looks into my eyes, her voice cracking as she says, "What if I moved myself? Would that make you happy?"

My heart pounds inside my chest so loud I can't hear myself think. "Don't say things you don't mean."

"But what if I do mean it? What if I admitted that this past weekend has been the happiest of my life? That being with you—being your fake girlfriend——is the most real I've felt in a relationship. That you give me more joy in our phone calls than anything else in my life, and I can't go back to living for fifteen minutes with you when I crave all your hours."

"Tess," I sigh out her name. "You can't uproot your life for me."

Sweetly, she replies, "I'm your Pixie. Tell me what will make you happy, and I'll do it."

My hands find her waist, and I stare down at her. *Is she serious? Could she really be happy here?*

"*Yes*," she whispers, knowing my thoughts before I voice them. "I could be the happiest here. Yes, you are enough for me…please, Ry, just tell me what would make you happy."

Leaning my forehead against hers, I hold her gaze and see the plea in her eyes.

"Please, Ry," she says again.

I shake my head. "Don't do that. Don't put my happiness ahead of your own."

"I'm just asking what would make you happy, Ry. And you promised me all your truths…"

"*You*. You make me happy. Your smile. Your laughter. The way you taste, your kindness, how you are with Erin—so open and loving. How tiny your hands are so we can always win at Jenga. The sounds you make when you come, the attitude you give me, both in and out of the bedroom. If I had to define happy, you would be the answer for me every time."

Her smile is big. "Ask me what would make me happy."

I shake my head. "Don't say it unless you mean it."

"Ask me, Ryan. Ask me what would make me happy."

I take a deep breath. "What would make you happy, Tess? What's your truth?"

"You," she whispers back as a tear slides down her cheek. "You're my truth. You're what makes me happy. *You*. You always say I put others first. That I worry about how to make everyone else happy. But it's not true. I'm selfish. Selfishly, I've clung to you for the last two decades knowing that our phone calls, our texts, our relationship, made me the happiest, even though I knew you were here, and I was there, and we couldn't be together."

I shake my head and rest my hand on her face, my thumb wiping her tears away. "I clung to them too." A shiver runs through me.

"I don't want to cling to the phone anymore though. I want to cling to you. I want *you*." Her words bring me a kind of joy I never knew was possible. A lightness I never thought I'd find.

"You do?" I ask honestly. I feel like maybe I'm delirious from my lack of sleep and I'm imagining this entire thing.

She laughs as she leans closer. "Yes, Ry. I don't want to be your fake girlfriend anymore. I want to be your real one."

I don't hesitate to pull her face to mine and kiss her. I know I must taste like smoke, even after a shower and a change of clothes. It will be days before the smell leaves, but she doesn't seem to mind. She groans as she deepens our kiss.

"Need inside you," I admit as I try lifting her shirt up.

Tessa laughs. "Aren't you tired? God, you must be starving too."

I shake my head. "Tess, I'm serious. I need you."

She winks at me. "Okay, Ry, but first we need to do a shot of tequila."

I laugh. "Why?"

She shrugs. "It's what I do. Work with me, okay?"

I kiss her again and then lean over her to grab the bottle. I untwist the cap quickly and then grab her wrist. "What are you doing?" she asks.

"Don't have salt and limes, so I'm gonna use you."

She smiles wide at the idea. That's something I know about Tessa. The girl is filthy in the bedroom, and I'm fucking thrilled about it. I hold the bottle out to her, and she opens her lips as I tip some into her mouth. She swallows, licks her lips, and then leans in and licks my neck. "Yum, smoky tequila."

I laugh and take a swig, the tequila burning my throat, and then I take her wrist and lick it, but I don't stop there. I put the bottle down and flip us so Tessa is on the couch and I'm on top of her. She yelps in surprise.

"What're you doing there, big guy?"

"I have a few more shots to do, so I need my salt," I say, as I slide her pants down, finding her bare. "Fuck, Tess, if I'd known you weren't wearing underwear…" I lose my voice as I stare down at my gorgeous girl. "You're so pretty."

Her saucy smile softens, and she whispers, "I'm so *happy*."

"You're so *mine*," I murmur as I lower myself between her legs and claim her. When I lick up her seam, she groans in satisfaction. "Hey, baby," I say, suddenly remembering something she said when we were at my sister's. "Tell me more about these adult books."

Tessa hums. "How 'bout I do one better? I'll read it to you, and you have to do everything it says."

My dick throbs in my pants.

"Oh baby, I think we can make that happen," I whisper as I alternate kissing and nibbling at her sensitive skin. "But tonight, I'm in control, because I gotta be honest—after I make you come, I'm sliding you onto my cock and fucking you how I've always wanted to."

She smirks at me, her red hair falling across her face and her lashes fluttering as she watches me eat her out. "Fuck, I love when you talk dirty."

I groan as I lick her again. "You taste so fucking good, baby." I reach for the tequila and pour a little onto her before licking it up, my tongue darting in and out of her pussy. Then I slide a finger in and watch her move. "You're so wet for me, baby. Is that because you want my cock? You want me to fuck you hard? Or should we go slow?"

"Hard," she pants as I crook my finger inside her and get back to work on her clit, where I alternate sucking and licking.

"I'm not going to last," she says.

I add another finger and lean up, watching her lips fall open, her hands dig into the couch, and her eyes close.

"Eyes open, baby. I want you to watch me control your body. I want you to remember what it looked like when I ruined you. Who's my good girl?"

She smiles as she bites down on her lip. "Me."

"You're mine, right, baby?"

"Yes, yes, yes!" she screams, squeezing her eyes shut as she pulses around my fingers.

I drop my head to her pussy and suck on her clit as she throbs.

"Fuck, Ry," she groans again and settles on the couch.

I slide my finger out of her, kiss her once more, and then lean up to look down at her. She's beautiful. Her face is soft and makeup free, beads of sweat dot her forehead, and her hair is damp at the edges, but she is the most beautiful I've ever seen her. Because she's mine.

Her eyes flutter open, and she smiles. "I need you, Ry."

I sit up and strip off my clothes, my cock standing in wait, then I lean over to offer her my hand. "Come here, baby."

Tessa sits up and pulls her top off, exposing her round, perky breasts, and I grab her and slide her onto my lap. As she presses against me, I feel her heat. I want in there so badly.

"Condom?" I ask her.

"I'm on birth control, and I get regular checkups."

I nod. "Me too, baby." My hand goes to her jaw, and I rub my thumb against it. "You're everything to me, Tess. I'm so sorry I made you feel anything—"

She stops me. "I don't want to talk about the past. We're good," she says as she leans in and kisses me. Then she pushes me back against the couch. "Now, I was promised a ride on this big, beautiful cock." She looks down and slides herself against me again, eliciting groans from us both.

"Kiss me through it," I say, knowing it's going to stretch her when she slides down. I want to feel her little gasps.

With her eyes on me and her hands on my shoulders, Tessa lifts herself up, and I position my cock so she can slide down. When the tip touches her, I take her lips, and then I use my hands to guide her hips down, her tiny gasps filling my mouth as we both adjust. Hot, tight pressure wraps around me, and she bites down on my lip as she finally accepts all of me.

"Fuck," she pants as she looks me in the eye and smiles. "I always called ya big boy, but damn, did you earn the nickname."

I laugh. She's got the best sense of humor. Then I relish in the sensation of her tightening around me with each twitch of my cock.

"I love you, Tessa," I say without thinking.

She gives me a soft smile. "Love you too, Ry. So much. Now fuck me before I get emotional and start crying again."

I chuckle. How can this woman turn me on and make me laugh at the same time?

Impatient with me, she puts her hand against my chest and pushes me back. "Fine, I'll do it." She rides me then, her tits bouncing, as she slides up and down and then grinds against me, seeking her own orgasm.

I lean up and grab a nipple in my mouth, pulling gasps and moans from her.

"I love how you look right now," she says as she continues to rock on me, both of us watching how my cock moves in and out of her.

"Truth, baby?"

She nods without slowing her rhythm.

"You've never been more beautiful than when you're riding my cock."

She laughs, and we kiss again and again until we're unable to talk, and only grunts and groans make it out of us. I smack her ass when she starts to slow, and she yelps in surprise and clenches around me, her orgasm almost instantaneous.

I come hard, holding her against my chest as I fill her.

She doesn't pull away from me when we're finished. Instead, she lies on me, quiet, and I run my hands through her hair as we sit together. "You're really staying?" I ask in wonder.

Tessa sits up and beams. "This is where I'm happy, Ry. Where else would I go?"

Epilogue

TESSA

Ryan and I spend the next few nights lost in one another and our days adjusting to our new normal. I fill him in on my plans to be bicoastal. I'm not ready to leave Boston, and with his family, I would never ask him to relocate. But I don't need to be in Boston regularly. I'll spend the majority of my time here and travel to meet with my editors, work on projects that need my in-person attention, and catch up with Grace and her little alien. But not until Grace gives birth. She needs me. Or at least I like to think she does. I'm pretty sure she and Cash will be back together and married within the year.

But Ry and I, we aren't talking about the future like that. I'm not even sure I want to be a mom, but what I do want is to be an aunt to his adorable niece, a friend to his sisters, a daughter to his mother, and Ryan's everything.

Speaking of that adorable girl, I've been spending every afternoon with her working on our children's book, which I pitched to one of my friends in publishing back when Ryan was being an idiot.

I've decided to give publishing a go. So once I'm ready to leave Boston and the magazine, my plan is to do that full time. My first book will be a children's one, but after that, quick and dirty is what I'm all about.

Ryan stares at me as he holds the ax in his hand, his flannel shirt open, and his long dark hair back in a man bun. "Is this really necessary?"

With my hands on my hips, I glare at him. "You promised to stay in character! You're my lumbersnack!"

Ryan looks toward the lake and shakes his head, his smile peeking through his scowl. "Baby, you're nuts. You know that, right?"

I flutter my eyelashes at him. "Very aware. Now hurry up and say your line so we can get the shot and make it back to your sister's to get ready for the wedding."

He rolls his eyes and then mutters the line as written.

"Ryan Manning! Say it like you mean it! I'm going to make this into a TikTok video to promote my book. You want me to be successful, don't you? Because if I'm not, I'll have to stay in Boston, and then you won't get all of this!" I shimmy my hips.

"Okay, Pix, I'll say the line." He laughs again. "God, I love you." He holds up the ax, swings it down into the wood, and looks back at the phone, hitting me with a smolder. "Wait 'til you see my other ax, baby."

I huff. "Ry, you aren't even trying."

"Tessa, this line is ridiculous. Can't I just swing the ax and look at you?"

"Only if you agree to do the video from the next scene in bed."

Ryan tosses the ax, runs at me, and grabs my phone. He sets it up on a tree as I scream, and then he pushes me back against another one. "How 'bout I make a video just for us, Pix?"

"From chapter nineteen?" I ask, my legs already clenching and my eyes wide.

He looks down at me and nods seriously.

"You'll really do that?" I ask in surprise.

"Tess, don't you get it? I'll do anything for you."

I wrap my legs around him and allow him to push me back against the tree, and with the camera rolling, he makes all my fantasies come true.

The wedding ceremony is held outdoors with lots of fire lamps, fur shawls to keep the guests and brides warm, and a dazzling view of the lake. Champagne glasses are kept full all night as we end the year with smiles, dancing, and laughter. Wearing the gold sequin dress he peeled off me every time I asked him to zip me up, I grip the two dollar bills I'd hidden in my purse and saunter up to my best friend.

"Dollar for your truths?" I tease my sexy boyfriend.

He looks oh-so-fuck-me hot in a black tux with his hair pulled back and his brown eyes molten for me.

He smiles as he licks his lips. "My truths belong to you. Don't need to pay for them, Pix."

"Are you happy?" I ask.

Ryan pulls me against his chest and then raises my chin so I'm looking right into his eyes as he admits, "I've never been happier in my life. But I'm scared this won't last. You'll go back, and we won't be able to keep this up—the back and forth."

"Ry, ask me for my truth…"

"What?"

"Ask me."

I see the concern on his face, but he has nothing to worry about. This is what we do. We share the truth, and as long as we're honest with each other, there is nothing to be afraid of. He'll share his worries and I'll extinguish them.

"Truth, Pix?" he asks, almost nervously.

"I'm *in love* with you."

Saying I love you isn't enough. We've loved each other our whole lives. This is different though. And he needs to know that, for me, this is it. *He's it.*

He blinks a few times, as if he needs me to say it again. So I do.

"I love you, Ryan Manning. I'm so fucking in love with you. It's crazy that we didn't do this decades ago. You don't have to worry about losing me because I've always been yours, and I'm going to make this work. You say I put too much energy into everyone else? Well, be prepared because all my fairy dust is gonna be aimed your way. I love you." I really can't stop saying it now that I've told him. It's like a dam has burst, and all the thoughts and feelings I've tamped down for years are flooding out.

He blinks again, and I can see the moment he settles into these words. As if his mind is saying, *she loves me, she really fucking loves me.*

"Did I break you?" I ask in a slow voice before reaching up to tap his forehead. "Anyone in there?"

He laughs. "Fuck, Pixie, I think you did."

I give him my full-watt smile. "So…was that too much of a truth for ya?"

He shakes his head in wonder and then lowers his lips to mine, kissing me softly. Against my lips, he murmurs, "Told ya I want all your truths, Tessa. Every single one."

"Feels good," I whisper against him.

"Wait," he says, "you need my truth."

I smile. "Okay, Ry, hit me with it."

"I love you," he croons, holding my chin as he speaks to my soul. He presses a thumb against my cheek and smiles. "I've loved you since we were teenagers. And I'll love you for the rest of my life. Whether you let me or not. You, Tessa Sanderson, are the *love* of my life."

"Hey, Ry," I say as tears well up in my eyes.

"Yeah, Pix?"

"It's midnight. Kiss me."

"Your wish is my command," he murmurs, leaning down and pressing his lips against mine.

I giggle softly against his mouth. "Actually, it was yours…" I hold up the dollar bill Shawn gave me.

His eyes crease in confusion. "Where'd you get this?"

My heart races as I admit, "Shawn said it fell down last week. The day I got here."

Ryan's face cracks open as I watch all the pieces fall into place. "So you replaced my wish?"

I shake my head. "Nah, but I did make my own."

He raises his eyes. "Yeah?"

I nod.

He looks down at the hopeful words scrawled in his handwriting.

I wish my best friend was my last first kiss.

"What was your wish, Pix?"

I read it out loud. "That yours comes true."

He smiles and drags me into his arms as he kisses me. When he pulls away, I see the fireworks over the lake reflected in his eyes.

Ryan murmurs, "Happy New Year, baby," then he turns around to the bar and points to Shawn, "Your turn, buddy! You have a wish to replace!"

SHAWN

I sweep up the confetti and sparkles, my mood a mix between grumpy and really fucking happy for my best friend. Ryan and Tessa are the type of couple you see together for the first time and wonder how they didn't realize they were meant to be together years ago. I couldn't be happier for him. I'm just tired of watching everyone else find someone while I'm…*stuck*. That's how I've felt since the accident.

I've been hiding here long enough. Ryan was right when he said I put my life on hold. But I don't think I can do it for another year. I need a change.

I shake my head as I stare at the black marker we keep on the bar.

I shouldn't.

But why not? It's worked for everyone else. What's the worst that could happen? I'm still here next Christmas? Still sweeping on New Year's?

With a growl, I grab the pen and slip a dollar out of my tip jar. With my tongue in my cheek, I write my wish.

I wish for something to mix up my life.

ARE YOU READY FOR SHAWN'S STORY?

PRE-ORDER A VERY MERRY MARGARITA MIX-UP NOW!

HTTPS://BOOKS2READ.COM/ AVERYMERRYMARGARITAMIXUP

A VERY MERRY MARGARITA MIX-UP

They say don't kiss your best friend. I accidentally kissed her twin sister.

Jules and Hailey Milsom couldn't be more different. Except they're identical twins.

One is my best friend. The other is the new girl in town, searching for a family she never knew existed.

It's just my luck that when I finally make a move on my best friend, I share the best kiss of my life with a stranger.

Any sane person would realize this is hopeless. But when the red-haired beauty needs a reason to stay in Bristol, I double down and try to make every one of her Christmas dreams come true.

And I kiss her…again and again.

But the one thing she really wants, a relationship with her twin, may be the one Christmas wish I can't deliver.

And this mix-up may be nothing more than a mistake.

ACKNOWLEDGEMENTS

This series was an absolute blast to write. Tessa literally wrote herself. She flowed so effortlessly after speaking to me through the Falling for Whiskey duet. But what made this experience even more special was that I was able to collaborate with wonderful authors to create a world where magic literally fell off the wall. That is kind of how this entire year has been for me. This book is releasing one year after my debut novel. In that period of time I have learned so much about this business and it is mostly through other authors, especially those who are part of this series. It all feels just a little bit like magic.

I wouldn't be where I am in my writing career if not for my team at Cover 2 Cover Author Services. Day in and day out you support me in this business and in life. I am beyond grateful.

To my Beta Readers, Katherine Jay, Cady and Meagan, thank you so much for your help in making Tessa and Ryan's story even better than when I gave it to you. And thank you for your friendship, you ladies are all something special.

And to The Cocktail Club, my street team and Tiktok team, you ladies literally make my day everyday with your excitement over my characters and these stories. You make this stressful business fun. Your excitement for my books surpasses my wildest dreams. Thank you!

A special thanks to Beth from VB Edits. I absolutely adored working with you on this book. Thank you so much for your help in bringing Tessa, Ryan and Shawn to the page.

Last but certainly not least, my readers, thank you so much for reading this book. I hope you enjoyed Shawn's perspective because his story is up next and I am thrilled to be heading back to Bristol Bay to visit Jack, Charlotte, Belle, Luca, CARMELLA, Amelia and Nate for Christmas in Bristol Bay. Shawn has been the dutiful bartender, the older brother and a pretty decent fake boyfriend, but I think it's finally time he got his happily ever after. I hope you enjoy it as much as I have enjoyed writing it.

If you want to follow along on my writing journey and have sneak peeks into all the characters in Bristol, follow me on Instagram, join my awesome Facebook group, sign-up for my newsletter and follow me on TikTok.

ALSO BY
BRITTANEE NICOLE

WHISKEY LIES (FALLING FOR WHISKEY BOOK 1)

He says I'm his soulmate. But I'm also another man's wife.

It was supposed to be a simple weekend away to forget the heartache caused by my cheating husband. But the man sitting next to me in 1B has different plans. Cash's whiskey-colored eyes and easy smile beg me to dance beneath the stars, kiss in the moonlight, and walk hand in hand down the streets of Boston. Unfortunately, life has other plans because I'm still married, and Cash James is the billionaire playboy standing between me and my dream promotion.

My job is simple—find Mr. James a wife. But nothing is easy when simply walking into his office and inhaling his woodsy scent makes me feel a buzz like I've just sipped straight from the whiskey bottle. He makes me tipsy with emotion. Breathless, fearless, and stupid.

Because no matter how good it feels in the moment, our love burns on the way down.

Whiskey Lies is book one of the Falling for Whiskey duet. It is a Billionaire Contemporary Romance. This book is part of a duet and is not a standalone.

LOVING WHISKEY (FALLING FOR WHISKEY BOOK 2)

All it took was one shot of whiskey to let myself burn.

Cash told me loving him wasn't a risk. He promised we would dance in the moonlight.

He swore he was nothing like the ones who broke my heart.

And he was right. He was so much worse.

But what do you do with an addiction you can't kick?

Drink in the shadows, take shots in the dark,
and savor the buzz knowing the next morning won't be worth it.
Because it's not enough.

Nothing is ever enough when the person you hate is also the one you love.

Loving Whiskey is book two of the Falling for Whiskey duet. It is a Billionaire Contemporary Romance.

This book is part of a Duet and is not a standalone.

SHE LIKES PINA COLADAS: A SECOND CHANCE ROMANCE (BRISTOL BAY BOOK 1)

Wanted: Hot Stranger For Vacation

It started with a simple message from the man known as Pina Coladas: Message me and Escape. After dumping my apartment-stealing boyfriend and rooming with my best friend's dog, the promise of fruity drinks, dancing in the rain, and maybe even a midnight romp, leaves me singing a familiar tune, excited to travel to the Azores with the stranger who answered my wanted ad.

When Jack, aka Mr. Perfect, aka the one who got away, shows up at the airport, I'm left to wonder if this is just another one of life's dirty pranks.

Jack isn't only hot, he's a fighter pilot with a sense of humor and blue eyes that make my butterflies dance. He's saying all the right things and sending sparks in every direction he looks, asking me to take all sorts of risks—like swimming in hot springs, jumping in mysterious pools, and giving him a second chance. But he still hasn't told me why he disappeared in the first place.

After a sip, or twenty, of sangria, I'll happily explore the cafés and the beaches and possibly even Jack's calves, but what I absolutely, positively will not do is fall for Jack—again.

Authors Note: She Likes Pina Coladas is a full-length, standalone, steamy and humorous contemporary read featuring a second chance at romance.

KISSES SWEET LIKE WINE : AN ENEMIES TO LOVERS OFFICE ROMANTIC COMEDY (BRISTOL BAY BOOK 2)

She's his boss. He wants her job. But he wants her more.

It started with a lie. An innocent, white lie. Okay, it wasn't so innocent. I'd hit rock bottom. No career, no boyfriend, and I had accidently moved into a fifty-five and up community where my best friend was a short seventy-year-old white haired Italian grandmother with big hips and an even bigger mouth who was constantly trying to set me up with her grandson.

When I was offered a job as a private investigator working with the hottest man I'd ever seen, I may have fibbed a little and told my new boss that I've got the right experience.

Tiny problem. I don't actually know what investigators do. Googling corporate espionage and taking my seventy-year-old neighbor on stings while drunk on Limoncello probably isn't in the job description. Neither is falling for my assistant, the gorgeous Green-Eyed Luca, who is either trying to take me down or take me out. I absolutely, positively cannot date Luca but with sparks flying, how could something so wrong feel so right? And will he still want me once he discovers the truth?

Authors Note: Kisses Sweet Like Wine is a full length, standalone, enemies to lovers, office romantic comedy in pink high heels, with a book boyfriend that will make you swoon, featuring explosive chemistry and a guaranteed happily ever after.

LOVE AND TEQUILA MAKE HER CRAZY (BRISTOL BAY BOOK 3)

Nate Pearson was my first everything.

My first friend, first love, and first heartbreak.

Now he's just my ex-husband.

It's been three years. It's time to let go of the past. When a man covered in tattoos walks into the bar where I work, with a guitar case slung over his back and a determined swagger, I think I'm finally ready to move on…until I see his guitar. I'd recognize it anywhere. It was the last gift Nate ever received from his father.

The man holding the guitar is different than the one I left behind in Nashville, but one thing remains the same, Nate Pearson will always be the love of my life.

The reasons why I asked for a divorce haven't changed. Only problem is, Nate Pearson says he still loves me, and this time he's playing for keeps.

Authors Note: Love & Tequila Make Her Crazy is a small town, brother's best friend, steamy, full-length, stand-alone, contemporary second-chance romance filled with emotion, that features both Nate and Amelia's past and present.

OVER THE RAINBOW (BRISTOL BAY BOOK 4)

I thought I learned my lesson...going undercover is not for me. But a trip to Positano with my favorite Italian grandmother wouldn't be complete without a stake-out and some prosecco. Now if I could just find my boyfriend and help the real detective locate the missing con artist, I can hopefully salvage this vacation.

Unless it's all just another elaborate scheme of Carmella's to help me get my happily ever after.

Made in the USA
Monee, IL
07 September 2023

42340154R00081